Victoria,

Never forget your love for horses, they are amazing creatures.

Reach for the stars and always remember that you can do anything you put your mind to!

Love always,
Jessica Marie Mauer

Wild Horses

THE BEGINNING

Jessica Gayle Maness

authorHOUSE®

AuthorHouse™
1663 Liberty Drive
Bloomington, IN 47403
www.authorhouse.com
Phone: 1-800-839-8640

First published by AuthorHouse 5/10/2011

ISBN: 978-1-4567-1413-0 (dj)
ISBN: 978-1-4567-1414-7 (sc)
ISBN: 978-1-4567-1415-4 (e)

Library of Congress Control Number: 2010918501

Printed in the United States of America

Any people depicted in stock imagery provided by Thinkstock are models, and such images are being used for illustrative purposes only. Certain stock imagery © Thinkstock.

This book is printed on acid-free paper.

This book is dedicated to my mom, who always believed in me and supported me, and my friends, who have hounded me to read this book for years, Levi Draper, Ricky Cardwell, and Carissa Elizalde. A special thanks is due to Mrs. Laura Orchard and Mr. Talesin McCall, my two most influential writing teachers. Sorry I didn't put ya'll in the book as characters.

Chapter 1

At dawn, as the first rays of sunlight softly kissed the bright green grasses of the Keswath Empire, the preparations for the birth of a child began. Yet, this was no ordinary child. The excitement filled every living being, with birds chirping their songs of joy, and horses prancing along the prairie. The air reverberated with anticipation of the arrival of the heir to the throne, an heir that, in prophecy, would right all wrongs.

The birth of the new princess of Empress Lahiik and Emperor Toki occurred in the beautiful palace called Ahab Palace. The Ahab Palace was two stories tall, had hundreds of rooms (in which each held a secret of its own), and stretched over an incredible distance, making it an even more awe inspiring sight. Outside there were pearly marble walls and golden peaks that seemed to stab into the heavens. The walls were etched with scenes of frolicking horses in the meadow. Their eyes were wide open and alert with their beautiful long tails flowing behind them, throughout their tails, carefully placed gold shavings – as if a flowing river of gold had replaced them. The scene in itself was intimidating, not even considering the size of the artwork.

Inside, the halls were wide and spotless, the walls and floors made of the finest Parian marble tiles, imported directly from the island of

Paros. The pure, white Parian marble was formed with no impurities such as sediment or sand inter-mixing with it during its formation. This made the marble less permeable.

Pictures of the past Emperors and Empress' covered the smooth, white walls. Every inch of the palace was lavished with the finest decorations, such as long flowing curtains, beautiful tapestries with scenes that took one's breath away at first sight, and small etchings of horses here and there, each with gold shavings inside, which sparkled exquisitely.

The main hall was filled with old antique furniture made of worn oak and birch wood and carpet made of the softest silk covering the floor. At the back of the main hall, a large fireplace stood, flames flickering and shining as dancing beams on the wall. The fireplace was made of dark, reddish brown bricks, with great tapestries hanging above. Inside the fireplace, the fire seemed to breathe, rising to the surface and then retreating back into itself continuously.

Every servant in the Ahab palace rushed through the halls, frantically trying to prepare for the arrival of the new princess. As Emperor Toki listened to the loud wailing of his wife, he paced nervously in the main hall, walking one way slowly and then quickly turning and walking the other way. He tried earnestly to clear his mind; it hurt him to have to hear his wife be in such agony during the throes of childbirth, as the shrill screams echoed through his thoughts.

Then, all of a sudden, fear overwhelmed him as unsettling questions began to weave their way into his chaotic thoughts. Will his princess be worthy of the crown? Is she truly meant to be the next queen? Is the prophecy really coming true? He considered these thoughts as he unconsciously watched all the servants running around, working as worker bees do in a hive.

Toki glanced out the large diamond shaped window at the guards, who were to alert him at the first sign of trouble. Sou Harra was growing impatient to get the throne, and feared the prophecy. Toki quickened his pace as he walked back and forth, as he kept a constant eye on the window, thoughts of Sou Harra sending chills down his spine.

A loud wail from Empress Lahiik pierced through Toki's thoughts, wrenching him back to the present situation. Toki winced and finally decided that he had endured enough torture for one day and, knowing there was nothing he could do for his lovely wife but get in the way of the midwife assisting the birth, Toki went outside for some fresh air.

Toki opened the door and squinted in the bright sun. He heard a soft cough and turned to consider the guard. "Sire," one of the guards formally greeted Toki, and then nodded toward the royal barn.

"The Stallion wishes to speak with you, sire." Toki glanced from the other guard towards the barn.

"Thank you. You may go along with your assignments." Toki looked away from the guards, curious as to what his old equine friend had to say.

Toki walked over to the royal barn, which was very near the palace. The barn had very few decorations, built more for its usefulness than its appearance, and instead of the brilliant marble that the palace was constructed of the barn was made only of plain willow wood, from the rain forest which surrounded the palace, serving as a natural barrier, a sort of protection that the gods seemed to have laid.

Toki quickened his pace and, in the anticipation of the moment, did not notice a large herd of wild horses off in the distance. The horses, a mixture of bays, duns, greys, palominos, pintos, roans, and paints, stood atop the hill with great elegance, watching over the events that were occurring at the Ahab palace.

Wild horses, with such power and strength, were protecting the royal family. Their powers included the ability to speak through their minds, and to send emotions into others thoughts, along with many other abilities that no one but wild horses could ever know of. The mares gave off a sense of protective instinct, worried glances flying in all directions around the Ahab Palace. If Toki would have looked up an instant before he reached the barn he may have seen the last mare departing, for the herd disappeared into the distance just as quickly as they had appeared.

When Toki reached the large wooden doors, he thrust them open. "You've finally come!" the stallion's voice echoed in Toki's mind in a tone that would have never been accepted by the Emperor had it been anyone else, but this was a horse who had been through it all with Toki. Anything was accepted by Toki coming from Satuu.

"Ah, so I have heard correctly. My old friend has returned. And I hope with good news?" Toki greeted him with a questioning glance. Satuu lowered his head and whinnied softly.

"I'm afraid not, Tokience." Satuu answered grimly. Toki's eyes widened.

"You have not called me by my true name since you brought the news that my father had died in battle. What is so important, Satuu?" Toki looked straight at the stallion, trying to read some kind of emotion. "How can this elegant, beautiful horse bring news worse than that of the death of my father," he pondered.

"I am not beautiful." Satuu's voice interrupted his thoughts. Toki gasped slightly.

"Wha…" Toki began, but Satuu interrupted.

"I am not beautiful. Beautiful is the sunrise and sunset. Beautiful is peaceful and enchanting. I am *not* beautiful."

Toki chuckled slightly. "Once again I forgot to shield my thoughts from you. Has there ever been a time that you stopped to consider that I am Emperor and usually I don't have to worry about my colleagues and friends probing my mind?"

"No. With all that has happened you should shield those thoughts of yours at all times." Satuu answered. Toki considered Satuu's wise words, but suddenly was brought to attention by a loud snort. "Enough polite conversation Toki! I have come to warn you that Sou Harra *will* come, maybe not now but he will. You must be careful. He wants power and yearns for the day that you pronounce the throne his. Do not underestimate him. He fears of the prophecy. He will not stop!" Satuu's worry rang through Toki's mind.

Toki kept silent. He tried to occupy himself and, desperately trying to hide the emotions that he knew played on his face, he fished for a brush and some fresh hay to relieve Satuu. "It must have been a long trip for you. Here," Toki offered some of the hay and Satuu took it gratefully.

Toki began to brush out the white stallion's brilliant fur. White as snow and thick as the rain forest, his fur, mane, and tail shone in a bright ray of sunlight that snuck through the cracked doors. When Satuu was finally comfortable and Toki's emotions were in check, Toki began, "Satuu, I understand your worries, but we have armies, we will withstand Sou Harra's attempts." Satuu let his head fall in frustration and snorted loudly.

"Don't you understand? He not only comes for your kingdom, but for all. You have read the prophecy, you know what will come. You must be prepared! Sou Harra is capable of much more than you allow yourself to believe, my friend." Satuu stomped his hoof and restlessly pranced around.

"Why do you speak of the prophecy? What are you trying to get at?" Toki demanded. A sigh reverberated through Toki's thoughts.

"It is nothing. Only know that you must be careful. Be ready for anything." Toki was puzzled. He began to wonder what Satuu was really trying to make him understand. Did Satuu know something that he didn't?

Suddenly, a servant ran through the large doors. "My lord, the child has arrived. Come, quickly!" And with that message the servant bowed slightly and ran back to the palace, not wanting to intrude on Toki and Satuu's conversation.

Toki stood up from his seat on the hay stack. "I shall see you soon then, old friend?" he asked Satuu.

"You may count on it."

After Toki and Satuu said their farewells, Toki briskly walked back up to the palace, his thoughts continually tormenting him, hearing Satuu's words as if he was still speaking. Everything that had just been exchanged left a sour taste in his mouth.

When Toki got back to the palace, the midwife met him before he could enter and see his child. "Sire, the birth took a lot out of Empress Lahiik. She has lost a lot of blood, also. She must rest." With a worried look, she let him in. "Oh and you will need to locate a wet nurse for the child." The midwife finished, being very discreet, for fear of worrying Toki too much, before ushering him in.

Toki took in every sight. The servants waiting patiently for orders in the shadows, the chairs strewn around the cot in which his wife laid, very still, with their baby girl in her arms. Her face was drained of color and sweat covered her body. She smiled faintly as she looked up at him. Her caramel colored eyes glowing with love.

Toki walked over to Lahiik. "How are you feeling?" Toki asked.

"Tired, but look at her, Toki. She will make a grand princess and an even grander queen!" Lahiik answered in a voice barely audible, her exhaustion very apparent.

"Yes, she will," Toki agreed, "But will everyone accept that," Toki thought to himself. He pulled a chair to himself and sat down beside Lahiik. He grasped her hand softly yet pulled away slightly at the feel of her hot skin.

He looked at her worriedly but then looked to their daughter and watched all his worries slip away, grasping his wife's hot, sweaty hand more tightly. The tiny figure of their daughter was silent and calm, pressed up against Lahiik's breast. Her tiny chest lifted and fell in harmony with that of Lahiik's. Toki sat there and merely watched the mother and daughter, a natural bond already formed.

Lahiik laid her head against the pillows and hugged the child closer, seeming as if she were worried that she would fly away with the small breeze coming in through the window.

Toki squeezed Lahiik's hand slightly, getting her attention. Lahiik nodded and slowly handed Toki the child's fragile figure. Toki smiled ear to ear as he looked down into the eyes of this beautiful child. He felt tears roll down his cheeks and hugged her close.

He felt as if his life had been completed. He had a beautiful wife, an even more beautiful daughter, and life seemed to be treating him well. Nothing seemed to be able to go wrong.

But it did.

Chapter 2

The next day troubles befell Empress Lahiik, troubles that worried everyone in the kingdom, so much that they all feared for her life. As Toki had gone to search for a suitable wet nurse, Lahiik had gone under an incredibly high fever, dehydration, and exhaustion and she now lay motionless in her bed, slipping in and out of a comatose state.

In the mean time, the midwife that had assisted the birth watched over the baby.

Toki quietly slipped through the door to the room in which Lahiik dwelled during her sickness. "Is she ok?" Toki asked the midwife when she looked up at the sound of footsteps.

"Truthfully, I don't know. The doctor just came in and said that her fever was much too high and that if we didn't get some fluids down her quickly, she could die. I'm sorry, sire, but, if I may be so bold, I doubt she will live through this tragic outcome of her labor. And even if she does live, she'll never be the same energetic Empress that I have come to know her as." The midwife felt very uncomfortable being so forward with the Emperor but knew that she should.

Toki's brow creased in frustration and he gasped as he realized that the midwife was right. He looked around, trying to find something to occupy himself and hide his tears that fought to fall.

Instead he took a deep breath and spoke to the midwife, "Thank you for watching our girl. The wet nurse should be here any minute to take her to the nursery." Toki tried not to dwell on the words the midwife had said just a moment ago.

"It is part of my duty to take care of the child for the first few days if the mother is not in fit condition." She answered standing and bowing her head slightly. She tried to relieve some tension from her neck.

Toki gazed into the distance, not seeming to be here or there. He felt lost in a world of depression. "So, what will you name the child?" the midwife asked, sensing the tension in the Emperor's shoulders.

Toki jumped in surprise, not really paying attention. "Huh? Oh, I don't know. It wouldn't feel right to name her without Lahiik awake and aware. But I know of a name that Lahiik and I loved so much. It is the name of my mother." Toki thought of his mother and tears welled up in his eyes.

The sad story of his mother's death filled his mind, but he pushed his emotions away. This was no time to break out into unnecessary tears, again. He took a breath and tried to control his emotions.

Suddenly he heard a small creak and turned around to see the wet nurse standing in the doorway, obediently. She was a small woman, about 5'1. Her dark hair was short, about shoulder length and she wore a small dark tunic.

Toki confronted the young woman and she spoke softly, "My Lord? I am here for the baby." The wet nurse silently slipped through the doorway and waited for him to gesture to take the child.

"Oh, yes. Come," he ushered her in to take the child. "Would you accompany her to the nursery?" Toki asked the midwife, in need of some time alone with his wife.

"Yes, sire, of course I will," she answered and followed the wet nurse out the door.

Toki waited till he was sure that he was alone with Lahiik, then walked over and knelt beside her. He watched as her steady breathing brought her chest up and down in smooth motions. He felt her forehead and recoiled at the feel of her hot skin.

"My Lahiik… You must get better. You just must." Toki said, yet knowing all along that she was unconscious and could not hear him. He grabbed a chair, sat beside her bed, and bowed his head, feeling one tear slide down his face.

Then he gazed up to the ceiling and said a silent prayer "Good god of this land, please spare my dear Lahiik. I don't know if I could live without her." He stayed there for what seemed like years, praying all the while for a miracle, hoping that somehow all the doctors were wrong, that Lahiik would miraculously recover. His tears fell nonstop now, and his fears welled up in his chest, choking away all hope.

"Toki, are you there?" A weak voice filled the air. Toki looked up in surprise to see Lahiik lying there, awake.

"Lahiik…" Toki started but couldn't organize his thoughts enough to say what he felt. All of his thoughts flooded in, everything he wanted to say to her was fighting to get out yet nothing came as he opened his mouth.

Instead he just looked into her eyes, glazed over with fever, hoping she would understand. Lahiik nodded, as if she knew how he felt. "I love you." She said, too out of breath to say much more.

"I love you, too." Toki answered and felt tears start to well up in his eyes once again. Toki closed his eyes to force the tears away. He had to be strong for Lahiik and if she saw his tears fall, she would be worried.

"The baby, how… How," Lahiik tried to ask but ran out of breath.

"She is fine. I have already located a wet nurse. Gloria is her name, I think, and the midwife is assisting her. They are in the nursery as we speak. Oh, Lahiik, you must see our daughter. It seems she grows every second." Toki said, grasping her hand and squeezing slightly.

"Lahiik," he began again but was afraid to talk too much. He mustered up his courage, for this may be his last chance. Tears slid down his face as these thoughts clouded his mind with anguish. Yet he still spoke with a clear voice, "Lahiik, what do you want to name our daughter?"

"De… Deba…" Lahiik tried to answer but couldn't. She just didn't have enough energy.

"Debace?" Toki finished for her. What a beautiful name, Toki thought, emotions battling inside him. Lahiik nodded tiredly.

Toki smiled a fake smile and brought himself closer to her. "Then that is that. The new princess shall be named Debace. Now, you should get some rest." Toki said, lightly kissing her on her forehead, and Lahiik abided to Toki's wishes. She really was quite tired.

Toki sat there, gaze fixed on Lahiik until her breathing slowed to signal that she was asleep. He jumped up out of his chair, which fell with a loud thud, and thrust his hands into the air, as if questioning the heavens. He looked around and spoke angrily, even painfully under his breath, "I have done nothing to dishonor any god! Lahiik has been nothing but loyal to all! Why do you do this to us? We've done nothing!" Toki gasped, surprised by the amount of emotion that carried out his voice and also scared he would wake up Lahiik.

"Nothing," he breathed, slumping down as he finally let his tears fall. He thought of his mother, of his beautiful wife, Lahiik, and the child that may end up motherless. "OH, Lahiik, please get better, we can get through this." He couldn't lose another person so close to him, not so soon.

The death of his mother had been too tragic and his heart was still mending from the sight of her mangled body, lying on the ground, a note attached to her chest. Her eyes were still opened and you could see the fear. What kind of person could do such a thing?

Not only was it cruel, but also would be quite a task. His mother was a strong character, and an even stronger Empress. She had saved the empire many times over and asked for nothing in return.

Her skills in magic and her knowledge were beyond any of the local wizards. Whoever had done this was on a mission, yet he knew who it was -- Sou Harra. But how, he did not know. However, one day he would, and that day was coming faster than he wished.

Toki fell to his knees and clutched his chest. He felt his heart break in two as he thought of the tragedies ahead and behind. But he had to be strong. He was Emperor. "I'm only human!" He thought. "But so are the people of my kingdom."

Soon he fell to a light slumber, there beside Lahiik's cot, with thoughts of death and anger still fresh in his mind.

When Toki awoke, he sat there entranced by a deep depression that was filling him. He stood up slowly from the softly carpeted floor beside Lahiik's bed. He stood there throughout the day, tears falling one after another, watching the woman he loved dying slowly.

His depression was apparent to many around him. "My Lord, you really should go outside and get some fresh air." Many nurses tried to convince him but he wouldn't budge.

Finally, at the request of Lahiik in the little time she stayed awake, Toki went to check on their daughter nearly a week after her birth.

He slowly walked down the hallway to the nursery. His body was sagging and his heart falling, breaking into a million pieces with each step as he thought of Lahiik's condition.

When he finally got there, he opened the door quietly and slipped in without anyone noticing. He looked around at the activity going on in the nursery.

Women ran around, chasing children of all different sizes. Families visited. Babies slept and cried and laughed. It was so joyful in this room that it lifted some of his dark mood.

"Emperor Toki!" Someone called to him, finally being noticed. He turned around and saw Gloria, the wet nurse that he had assigned the job of caring for his baby girl until Lahiik was better.

"*If she ever does,*" a cold voice said inside his thoughts, wiping any spark of happiness away from his thoughts.

He walked over to Gloria. "Sire, how is our young Empress?" she asked when he made it to her.

"Not well" Toki answered, lifting up his hand as if to wipe away the thought.

"Oh, well, have you thought of a name yet?" she quickly changed the subject.

"Yes. Debace. That is what Lahiik wants." He said. Gloria nodded in approval.

"Very pretty name. Perfect for the beautiful angel I hold in my arms." She answered, glancing down at the baby. "Would you like to hold her?" She held the tiny infant out towards Toki.

Toki nodded and took her carefully in his arms. He held her, careful to hold her head, and looked deep within her eyes, wishing to leave behind the depression of life. "She shines like the morning stars," Toki thought, "Debace is a perfect name for my little shining star."

Toki stood there, looking into Debace's eyes, as everything else seemed to melt away. His feelings of sorrow, anger, fear and hate disappeared in an instant. Even the people around him seemed to just be a figment of his imagination as he stared at this beautiful baby girl.

Then, something in her eyes gave him a feeling, like some burden had been lifted from his shoulders. Something seemed different as he stared into those soft brown eyes. He felt a warmness blossom inside him and heard a soft whisper in his mind, "It's ok."

Debace giggled and grabbed for his nose. Toki let a small gasp escape his lips; then, a small tear rolled down his cheek. Not like those of sorrow he had been shedding in these last 7 days but a tear of joy. He knew everything would be alright just as the whisper had said.

After Toki had left the nursery and was on his way back to the room where Lahiik dwelled in, a doctor ran to him. "My Lord, you must come! Something has happened to Empress Lahiik!" he exclaimed urgently.

Toki raced down the hallway, fear clear on his face. "What could have happened now," he thought as he ran as fast as he could down the wide hall.

When he finally reached the door he hesitated at opening it. "My god, *please*, let her be alright." He said aloud as he twisted the handle.

But what he saw surprised him more than anything.

There, in the middle of the large room, was Lahiik, standing and smiling. She ran to Toki and thrust her arms around his neck, "Toki! Look! I'm cured. By the gods' graces, I'm cured!"

"She *ran*," he thought

"How.. Wha…" he started but was just so happy that she was ok, that he pulled her tighter in their embrace.

"My Lahiik is ok. She is ok!" He thought, jubilantly. Lahiik squeezed him even tighter.

She raised her head to his ear and whispered softly, "When I was asleep I heard a voice. It said it would be alright, that I was meant to take care of our Debace." Her smile faded ever so slightly, "But it also said that the prophecy would come true, and then a large black mare walked through the mist to me. Toki, a black mare, what does it mean?"

Toki looked at her face and saw the worry in her eyes. "It means nothing, just that you're ok." He lied, but clearly knew what it meant. He had heard what the prophecy said. Yet, he refused to believe it.

Chapter 3 (5 yrs later)

Toki watched through the large diamond window as Lahiik and Debace ran around chasing each other and laughing. He sighed in relief. "Peace." He whispered. "Peace at last."

Ever since the birth of Debace, activities around the Ahab Palace had been hectic. He had to tend to every day things along with making sure Debace was out of trouble and assigning people to different jobs. Luckily he had Lahiik. "Lucky indeed," he thought as he remembered when he had nearly lost her. If it wasn't for miracles, he probably would have lost her, too.

He stood there contemplating the past years of his life as a father, Emperor, and husband, until a servant suddenly walked up; she bowed her head, cleared her throat, and aroused Toki from his thoughts.

"My lord, good day to you," the servant greeted him with a slight bow.

"And you. What brings you Shiren?" Toki asked. He was curious to what had brought her to the palace, as she usually worked with the peasants in the fields.

"Sire, it's the stallion again! Satuu, I mean. He requests your presence. If it's not too bold of me, I think he is quite anxious, Sire. Do you think something is going on?" She asked as she slipped out of the formality of a servant speaking with her Emperor into the speech of old playmates.

"It is possible." Toki said calmly, trying not to let the thoughts of panic enter his mind. "Thank you, Shiren." He said as he turned away from her and opened the door, starting his trek to the royal barn.

Debace and Lahiik looked up in surprise at the sound of the door opening. "Father, where are you going?" Debace asked, her smile of glee disappearing from her face when she noticed the intense emotions playing on her father's face.

"To the royal barn," he said promptly, hurrying to avoid any more questions. He didn't want to worry Debace nor Lahiik and if he told them that Satuu was there, they would know something was wrong.

Lahiik's smile slowly fell into a frown as she noticed Toki and his eagerness to get away. "Debace let your father go on with his business," Lahiik said sternly.

"Yes mother," Debace quickly ran back to Lahiik. Lahiik wrapped her arms around her and held her close. She looked towards Toki as he rushed off and wondered what could have possibly happened that he was being so guarded about.

Thankful for Lahiik's understanding of the urgency of the moment, Toki quickly walked to the barn, trying not to seem too disturbed.

He finally made it to the barn, hesitated only a moment, then swung open the large doors, expecting to see only Satuu, but was caught by surprise when he saw the large skeletal figure in the shadows.

Toki walked inside after shutting the doors behind him. He looked questioningly from Satuu to the skeletal figure and back to Satuu. "Toki, the time has come." Satuu said gravely, his voice echoing in Toki's already troubled thoughts.

"For what, my old friend?" Toki asked but clearly knew the answer.

"We have come to warn you of the arrival of Sou Harra. He can wait no longer and he is not willing to risk the throne and wait to see if

Debace grows to be a suitable queen. He is coming and he isn't coming to talk." Satuu explained.

Toki risked a quick glance at the figure in the shadows before replying to this piece of terrible news. "I know." He finally answered, knowing he had to embrace the bitter truth. "Yes, I know what I must do, but I just can't," he thought.

He walked slowly to sit down so he could think over the times to come. A long silence settled until Satuu finally broke through his thoughts, asking "Have you been training her for her destiny?"

Toki looked up, startled, "Huh, oh. Yes I have. She has learned to ride a horse for long periods of time and even started to learn how to brandish a sword." He thought back to the first day Debace and he had sparred.

Toki slumped and looked down from Satuu to his feet. Satuu waited, noticing a look on Toki's face that revealed more was there than what was being said.

Finally Toki raised his gaze and began, "Satuu? I don't know if I can do it. I can't give her up. It is impossible." Toki turned his head, trying to hide the tears that he knew had fallen.

He sat there, head turned, until he had his emotions under control. Satuu waited for Toki to collect himself. "Toki, I understand what you're going through but you must let me take her with me. If you don't, she will surely die." Satuu echoed a sigh of remorse, yet stood strong on the subject. "Toki, I am your friend. You have known me since we were both young and in that time, we have learned to trust and respect one another. Toki, listen to me. As your friend and as your battle companion, trust me when I say, it is for the best. You must let me take her with me to…"

Suddenly, Toki heard footsteps behind him and a shout, "Stop!" the figure stepped out of the shadows.

Toki looked around to see a beam of light sneak through a crack between the slightly opened doors. He wondered at how this could be for he was sure he had shut the doors securely.

The skeletal figure walked briskly to the entrance of the barn.

When he reached the entrance he snatched a small child from a corner and dragged her roughly to Satuu.

He threw her to the ground and began an incantation of the Old, but before he could finish Toki thrust his hand towards the man. "What are you doing? Let my daughter go!" he demanded as he quickly pulled up Debace from the ground.

"Father, I'm so sorry. I didn't mean to…" she began as she frantically begged for her father's mercy. Toki held her shoulders and watched her scared face.

"Debace, what are you doing in here? Why did you…" Toki stopped and quickly scanned her over. "You! Who do you think you are to drag a princess around like she's a peasant? Did you not recognize your own princess? How dare you!" Toki blew up at the stranger.

He raised his hand and began an incantation of paralysis until Satuu stopped him, walking in between the two.

"Toki!" he hissed sending a sharp shock through Toki's thoughts. "Why do you take such drastic measures? He is merely trying to protect us." Satuu raised his voice. Toki winced at the sound of disapproval in his voice.

Toki calmed his simmering anger and held his daughter close with his arm on her back. "Who is this stranger?" he asked with a hint of anger still lingering in his voice.

The figure stepped forward and addressed Toki, "I am Cohilla, protector of the rain forest. Satuu has requested that I be here to help with the…" he hesitated and looked at Debace before continuing, "transition," he finished, returning back to the shadows before anymore questions arose.

"What do you mean, transition?" Debace asked, hugging closely to Toki. Cohilla raised one hand and she fell silently on the floor.

Toki fell to the floor with her and gathered her into his arms. "What did you do?" Toki demanded with venom clear in his voice.

"She is merely sleeping. She will wake soon enough." Cohilla replied with the same venomous voice.

A quick incantation played at the end of Toki's tongue. "Toki, enough of these arguments," Satuu warned.

"If he is a protector then why didn't he put a ward on the barn, so that unwanted ears couldn't hear?" Toki jumped at the chance to criticize Cohilla.

"I did. Somehow, she got through." Cohilla declared. Toki glared at Cohilla. He barely remembered that his daughter was in his arms before he stood. He softly set her on the floor near a pile of hay to rest her head and approached Cohilla, his anger overflowing.

Toki stood there, face to face with Cohilla, and glowered at him. Oh the horrible things he wanted to do to this man, if he could be called a man at all. Many painful spells played at the end of his tongue, but he held back. This was a protector of the rain forest after all, and any protector of the rain forest could counter a spell from a mere Emperor.

He looked down at Debace and was lost in thought once again. "If only she got her talents sooner," he thought, "Then she would have the ability to protect herself."

He suddenly thought of his mother. How strong she was in the power of weaving spells and incantations to meet her needs. She was said to be stronger than any other and she cast every spell with the grace of a well trained sorceress. "But," he remembered, "she wasn't a sorceress. She was merely an Empress, a beautiful one at that. Her death was a tragedy to all."

Tears pushed from behind Toki's eyelids and he sat down beside Debace.

"Toki, we must begin preparations. We don't have much time." Satuu rushed as he roused Toki from his sorrows.

"Yes, of course." Toki replied and he rose to his feet. "You will need extra food and water." Toki glanced over his shoulder as he grabbed the saddle from its place.

He walked over to Satuu, saddle in hand, and tried to push every emotion from his thoughts. This was a time of need for his daughter and he couldn't risk breaking down again. Debace needed him.

Toki laid the saddle over Satuu's back and had begun to strap it down when Debace arose from her sleep. "Father?" she asked shakily as she tried to gain her balance on her feet.

"Debace, come here," Toki gestured for her to come over to him. Debace cautiously walked to her father. "Debace, I have some things that I must tell you. I have waited much too long to tell you the truth."

And so he told her about Satuu's identity and about how Sou Harra wanted her dead and, most importantly, he told her about the long journey she had to make and the hardships she would most likely endure. When he finally finished he began tightening the straps on the saddle again.

Debace looked up, confusion etched on her face. "Father, does that mean I must leave you? I won't! I just can't." she cried sadly.

"Debace, you must. You have to be strong." Toki said, trying to keep his emotions under control.

"But..." Debace began but Cohilla stepped forward.

"Debace, you are princess. The heir to the throne and this empire needs you." He stopped and waved a light hand over her head. "This will protect you." He said and then stepped back.

Debace felt a light wind blow her hair and surround her. She marveled at this but quickly hugged her father, tears streaming down her face. This might be the last time she ever sees her father, and she intended to remember it.

Chapter 4

"Sire, Sou Harra is here!" a servant burst through the doors to report the news and then ran back to the palace.

Toki grasped Debace by her shoulders and knelt beside her, kissing her cheek. Then he hugged her tightly. "Quickly! Debace, get on Satuu's back and ride into the sunset."

Debace gasped and shook her head, backing away from her father. "No, I don't want to leave you."

Toki brought her close and hugged her once again. "Debace, I love you dearly. And that is why you must go. There is so much more than just whether you or I are ready for this. You must go."

Debace felt tears well up in her eyes. "Ok." She whispered. Debace walked to Satuu and began to climb up into the saddle.

Toki stood beside Satuu, the commotion around him fading away as he realized that he would never see his daughter again, he felt she had barely come into his life.

"Yet she had," he thought. Merely 5 years ago he had picked her up and looked into her beautiful eyes and felt that peace; and now he looked into those same eyes again feeling that peace. Then suddenly the reality around him flooded his thoughts.

"Cohilla, you stay with me and help protect my kingdom! I will NOT surrender to Sou Harra," Toki began giving orders.

As Debace collected herself and grabbed the reins, Toki and Cohilla were at the door fighting off some of Sou Harra's soldiers. Satuu accelerated toward the door and Debace tightened her grip on the reins.

Debace closed her eyes as they burst through the door and the large group of people blocking it. She opened her eyes as they burst into the sunlight outside and turned at the sound of a woman screaming.

"Mother!" Debace screamed as she watched a large soldier grabbing her mother and throwing her to the ground.

"Don't look back, young one. It will only be harder to leave." Satuu advised, as he ran on, running from the horror of the scene.

Satuu gained speed as the majority of Sou Harra's army and many of his sorcerers trailed behind them. Debace risked a glance behind her and saw her father and Cohilla being overtaken. "First my mother, then my father! I can't just leave them like that," she thought as she loosened her grip on Satuu.

"Satuu, turn around! I can't just leave them to be killed." Debace demanded.

"No." Satuu replied plainly, too occupied by trying to outrun the army and dodge spells.

"TURN AROUND *NOW*!" Satuu jumped at her shrill voice and succumbed to her power.

Debace thought of every cruel thing ever thought of, directing this to the army, and tracked down her parents. "I may have to leave them, but I won't leave without a fight," she thought.

She reached for her side where her sword usually lay but only found her bare side. "Oh, no, I left my sword!" she yelled over the increasing noise of beating hooves.

She thought of the day her father gave her that sword, tears welling up in her eyes.

Then, she realized the new sounds. "What is that?" she asked and found out when she looked behind her.

There, right behind them, was a huge herd of beautiful horses. They

22

accelerated and reached Satuu's side, soon passing him and blocking their path which was heading straight for Sou Harra and his army.

"NO!" Debace yelled as Satuu turned back around and she watched as two soldiers dragged her mother and father harshly across the ground. She quickly turned her head when she saw the horrific look on her mother's face as one of the soldiers drew their sword.

Tears fought to be free but Debace wouldn't let them pass her eyes. This wasn't a time for sorrow. She had to get out of here.

The herd of horses surrounded her and Satuu as they galloped ahead.

An abrupt stop revealed a large gorge in their path.

"Ah hah, they're trapped! Hurry you buffoons! GET HER!" Sou Harra ordered.

Satuu backed up looking at the gorge with apparent intent. Then he ran, full speed, right toward the gorge.

"Satuu!" Debace yelled when she finally figured out what he meant to do. She hugged close to Satuu's neck and closed her eyes, sure her life was about to come to an abrupt end.

She waited and waited for what seemed like a millennium, until she finally looked up. They had made it!

She looked behind her, expecting to see the herd of wild horses behind them but only saw Sou Harra, desperately trying to find a way across the gorge, and his army, awaiting the orders from their leader. "You can run all you want, but I will get you!" Sou Harra screamed in his frustration.

Debace turned back around to watch where they were going but an instant later she felt so exhausted and soon lay there unconscious on Satuu's back. Her last thought was the look of horror on her mother's face and her sorrow of having to leave them to their death.

Chapter 5

When Debace finally awoke, she discovered that they were in the middle of a dense, humid rain forest. Under the large canopy of leaves, there was little sunlight and the hot, humid air made it hard to breathe.

"Satuu? Where are we?" Debace asked, swallowing hard as she remembered what had exhausted her so.

"The rain forest that surrounds the palace; we should make camp soon." Satuu slowed his pace and knelt down so that Debace could begin to try to take off the saddle.

She jumped off and started loosening the straps, while Satuu lay on the ground to make it easier. "This is heavy!" Debace exclaimed as she tried to pick the saddle up off Satuu's back to carry it to a fallen tree trunk she had noticed.

"Concentrate and you shall move it. Use your magic," Satuu said tiredly as he laid his head on the damp ground.

"Satuu, I don't have magic! My father can say words to do something but I can't! It's just impossible," Debace furrowed her brow in frustration.

"Yes you do. As the 2nd generation of Debace Ke Swathiana, you have her ability. I would help but I am simply too tired. Try," Satuu told her before he drifted into a soft slumber.

Debace sat there, confused. "I don't have powers! Father said so," she thought, trying to figure out what was actually true.

When she failed for the third time, she nearly gave up, but something told her to keep on trying. She stared at the saddle, thinking of it floating in the air and pushed all thoughts away from her mind.

She began to get frustrated and said a small curse that she had said since she first began to talk, even though her father had strongly advised her to do otherwise.

"Se Empeir Gaz thunta," Debace turned her head away from the saddle, but she couldn't get her thoughts away from the saddle.

She slowly looked back at the saddle and expected to see it just sitting there on the ground but instead saw it floating in the air. A small gasp of surprise escaped her lips before she tried to move the saddle to the log.

"Satuu was right!" she whispered softly as she watched the saddle slowly move from its place in the air and onto the log.

Debace walked over to the log and lifted her hand toward it. "This is impossible."

She hesitantly grabbed the saddle bag from the side of the saddle and got a blanket her father had packed. "Father..." Tears began to stream down her face.

She walked over to Satuu and leaned against his stomach, laying the blanket across Satuu and herself, and, as the night chilled to a cold, silent darkness, she slept.

Debace opened her eyes and lay very still on the cold, damp ground. What had awakened her so abruptly? The air around her seemed musty and, then, she realized that Satuu wasn't beside her. "Where could he be," she thought.

She quickly scrambled to her feet and scanned her surroundings. What was going on? Why did it seem so quiet?

She caught a glimpse of color in the trees surrounding her and slowly walked toward it. Something was there.

Suddenly, Satuu was right in front of her. "We must leave, NOW!" The urgency in Satuu's voice rang through Debace's cloudy thoughts. Satuu waved his head toward the saddle and it flew to his back and gracefully landed in the middle of his back. "Hurry, Debace! Tighten the straps. We must get out of here," Satuu urged her to quicken her pace.

As Debace started to tighten the straps under Satuu's belly, she listened carefully for any strange noises. Then she heard it, the sound of feet moving through the damp undergrowth of the rain forest floor and voices. She quickly grabbed all their supplies and scrambled onto Satuu's back.

"Hang on tight!" Satuu said as he raced in the opposite direction that the voices were coming from. Debace grasped his mane and the reins and held on tightly.

The voices were getting louder and louder. She turned around and saw that same face that depicted horror. Sou Harra. "It's him, Satuu! Oh please, Satuu, get us out of here."

Satuu just nodded his head and raced even faster through the forest.

Debace ducked her head as she dodged stray limbs. Dew from the trees spraying in her face.

"There they are! Sorcerers, get them, dead or alive."

She heard Sou Harra shout orders. Suddenly, she felt anger well up inside her and she looked around for some kind of weapon. Then, she saw a discolorization in the air and the same elegant and graceful herd of horses appeared that had protected her and Satuu at the palace.

The lead looked at Debace and nodded toward her hands. Debace looked down and saw sparks of magic playing at the end of her fingers.

"Pay back time," She yelled and turned around and shot deadly spells toward the army following them.

"Where did that come from?" she heard Sorcerers exclaim. She fed her anger and with that fed the magic she possessed. She hit two Sorcerers and they instantly fell on the ground.

She aimed for Sou Harra and let out a loud roar of triumph as she saw that the spark had hit its target. Sou Harra staggered before yelling a retreat and then turned and fell to the ground.

Debace dropped her hands and looked in front of her as Satuu raced on. She glanced around and watched as each horse disappeared as if they were a figment of her imagination.

Satuu slowed as they reached the end of the rain forest, into a meadow and walked out toward a small house with a large barn.

Chapter 6

*A*s Satuu neared the house, an elderly woman appeared from behind the barn. "Who are you and what do you want?" the woman yelled.

Satuu continued without saying a word and cautiously approached the woman. Debace felt a tugging at the end of her thoughts and yelled back, "We're not here in hostility." She mused on the word hostility. "What does that mean? Well, always worked for Father, maybe it'll work for me, too," she thought.

When they finally reached the elderly woman, Debace studied her features. She was barely taller than Debace, herself, and had wrinkles that showed a hard life. She had brown eyes that showed wisdom and tanned skin that revealed hard work. By what Debace could tell, she was just an ordinary farm woman.

Debace hopped off Satuu. She watched as Satuu stared at the old woman. Suddenly, the old woman's eyes flew open in surprise and she began to sprint into the house.

When she came back out, she was accompanied by a younger woman that was much taller than the old woman. The elder woman was ranting on and on and the younger one raised her hand and said, "Mother,

29

please go inside. It is alright. I'm sure that you made a mistake." Her mother lowered her head and went into the house.

"Satuu? Is that you?" the young woman asked, directing the question toward Satuu. "Yes, Beatrix. How have you been?" Satuu asked, tiredly. Debace jumped slightly when she, too, heard Satuu's voice in her mind.

"Satuu! You must have been gone for years! I am fine but you nearly gave my mother a heart attack. How many times must I tell you that she doesn't understand?" She ran to Satuu and threw her arms around his neck.

As the two embraced, Debace felt that she had gone unnoticed. "Good, I need some time to myself. Maybe I can slip away," she thought as she bit at her bottom lip and tried to silently slip away from the two.

Before she could get past them, Beatrix caught her eye, "And who might this be?" She threw an arm around Debace's shoulder and brought her closer to examine her.

"Beatrix, we must..." but before Satuu could divert her attention she recognized Debace.

"Satuu! This is Debace Ke Swathiana? Why is she here?" She nervously glanced around, taking a step away from the young princess.

"Beatrix, I need your help. We need to rest. Sou Harra and his army have been tracking us for the last 3 days. I can't go much longer without rest and I'm sure that goes same for Debace. Please, will you provide for us?" Satuu asked.

Beatrix pondered her options. Either she turns down her friend or she lets him stay with her, but she knew it was more complicated than that.

The dangers that would come were numerous.

She finally decided, "Yes, Satuu. I promised I would stay with you till the end and I will. Come, I will fix up the apartment in the barn for you."

She gestured for them to follow her and walked toward the house.

Debace looked up at the sky and saw the sun begin to set, the oranges and pinks blending together brilliantly. She felt as if she was in a dream, but this dream was interrupted by the growling of her stomach.

"Beatrix? I'm really hungry." She said as they walked.

"Yes, of course." Beatrix whispered.

Debace walked along side Beatrix and Satuu and studied the difference between her mother and this beautiful woman. "Mother," Debace thought sadly.

She pictured her mom in her mind. They both had long, beautiful brown hair that seemed to flow on and on. Her creamy chocolate eyes didn't even measure to Beatrix's dark brown eyes.

"They almost seem black," Debace examined.

Both women had a strong stance with a light understanding expression always upon their face.

"How could I leave her? Mother," Debace pushed tears away from her face as they fell silently, slowing her pace to fall behind Beatrix and Satuu. When she had recovered herself, she caught up with Satuu and Beatrix.

When they finally reached the house, Beatrix led them to the barn where, in the back, there was a neat little apartment.

"You can stay here for the night." She said and she ran into the house and came back with some fruit and vegetables. "I'm afraid this is all we have," She proclaimed and rushed out after laying it on the table and saying a quick "goodnight".

Debace picked up an apple and lay down on the bed. Before she even realized it, she was fast asleep, still holding the apple.

Debace awoke before the sun had even begun to rise. She looked around to see where Satuu was and discovered him beside the bed she was sleeping on. She quietly got up to get a drink of water and go to the restroom.

When she returned to the bed, Satuu was awake also. "How did you sleep?" Satuu asked. Debace sat on the bed and grabbed the apple that had fallen from her hand.

"Good enough." She replied as she stuffed her mouth with the juicy apple. She wiped her mouth with the back of her hand and looked up, "Satuu, will I ever have a peaceful night again?" she asked.

"I truly don't know." Satuu replied.

Debace lowered her head. "My dreams... they were filled with scary thoughts and my parents. Oh, my mother... Do you think she is ok?" Debace fought to hold back the tears, but failed.

"I hope so." Satuu said, sadly.

Debace looked at Satuu with pleading eyes. "What is happening to me? Where are we? How will I ever get back? Oh, Satuu. I'm so scared. Why me," She began to sob.

"You are finding out the truth and soon you will know more. You are too young to understand too much now but you will know, but it is ok to be scared. You're merely a child and shouldn't have to deal with this but what's done is done. It may be because you are the princess and have responsibilities but why now, I truly don't know." Satuu laid his head down. How strong this young girl seems. She is only 5 years old and has already mastered a very difficult spell for one of her age.

Debace lay down and tried to sleep. She needed rest if she would go much farther. "Oh mother, Oh father! I love you," she thought as she drifted into a restless slumber.

When Debace finally woke again, the sun was just rising. She sat up and waited for her eyes to adjust to the light that was showing through the slightly opened doors.

When she could see better, she got up, went to the sink, and washed her face. Then, she slowly dried her face with her shirt and walked outside.

The sun had risen just over the horizon and cast a golden glow upon the land.

Debace looked around for Satuu and decided to walk up to the house. When she got there, she heard voices. "Beatrix, we must leave. Thank you for your hospitality but Sou Harra is coming and I can't risk him getting a hold of the child. Be careful." She heard Satuu's voice, echoing silently in her thoughts.

"What is so important about this one child? Why would Sou Harra chase you all the way through the rain forest?" She heard Beatrix ask.

"Because, Debace is the..." suddenly, Satuu stopped and looked straight where Debace was hiding. Debace gasped slightly and sat still, making herself as small as she could.

Satuu caught Beatrix's eyes one last time before heading toward the barn. Debace attempted to allow her thoughts to spread toward them, hoping to hear Satuu's voice, but only heard silence.

Debace sneaked to the barn and found Satuu standing there, waiting.

"Do you enjoy eavesdropping?" he asked, softly.

"No, I just..." Debace walked over to the saddle and began to drag it toward Satuu. "This is heavier than the first time I tried to pick it up. Satuu, can you help me?" she asked.

Satuu went over to the saddle and lay beside it. Soon it began to float until it was on Satuu's back.

Debace strapped it down and wondered what Satuu was going to say before he had noticed her there, but when she mustered up enough courage to bring it up Satuu would just change the subject.

When they were finally ready to go, Debace jumped onto Satuu's back and they went to say their farewells to Beatrix.

"Satuu, hurry! Sou Harra has just exited the forest." Beatrix rushed him. Satuu reluctantly began to trot.

"Good bye!" Satuu yelled behind him as he finally raced toward the horizon. "Be careful." He said quietly as he ran faster.

Beatrix watched until it seemed they had disappeared into the horizon, until a soft, cold, wet hand landed on her shoulder.

"Mother," She said, not turning right away to face her. Beatrix grabbed her hand and flinched at the cold clamminess. She slowly turned around.

Standing there, blood dripping down her face from the gash on the top of her head, was her mother.

Suddenly, she fell to the ground and Beatrix fell with her, catching her and laying her bloodied head on her lap.

"Beautiful, isn't she?" Beatrix heard a cold voice say from above her.

She looked up and saw the cruel face of Sou Harra. "You monster!" She pulled her mother's head closer to her.

Sou Harra chuckled and snapped his fingers. Two pairs of hard hands grasped Beatrix's arms and dragged her away from her mother. The men dragged her hands behind her back and clasp cold iron on her wrists.

"You won't get away with this! You have no right!!!" Beatrix growled.

"Actually I do. You have been accused of treason against the Empire, by helping that little brat." Sou Harra grinned viciously.

"You have no authority! And that little brat is our princess. I would give my life for her!" Beatrix screamed.

"Oh, will you? I will see to it that your wish be granted. Oh, didn't you hear the good news?" Sou Harra said with a slight giggle, with enough venom in his voice to scare even an Altura. "*I* am Emperor now!" He snapped his fingers again and the soldiers dragged Beatrix to a large boulder, pushed her to her knees, and lay her head on the boulder.

Satuu stood on the horizon and watched the tragic events down below. He panicked as he saw what the soldiers were preparing to do, but merely watched helplessly as the huge soldier brought down his sword, soundlessly ending the life of a friend.

Satuu felt helpless, for if he tried to help, then he would be putting Debace in danger. Debace was the future, a future that would come with sacrifices. "Good Bye." He thought and turned to run, coming closer to safety all the time.

Chapter 7

"Satuu? Where are we?" Debace asked, tiredly, slowly picking up her head.

"We aren't too far from the Altura's lands." Satuu answered, his voice softly reverberating in Debace's mind.

Debace sagged in the saddle seat. It had now been at least 1 week since they had left the palace and, oh, how tired she felt. She had never been gone from the palace for this long since her and her father had gotten lost in the rain forest just last year.

Nothing could measure to the exhaustion she felt now. Debace closed her eyes quickly to block her tears from falling as she thought of her father and tried to divert her attention. "Satuu, these Alturas don't sound very nice. Besides what is so important about getting to them?"

Debace began to become somewhat frightened, and finally forgot her sad thoughts, looking too much now into the future. Too many other dangers had she encountered and too many that she had not yet.

Satuu slowed his pace. "Alturas aren't any different from the servants that ran around the palace. The only difference is their appearance and temper. Anger an Altura, and it may well be the last thing you do. But do not be frightened. Your father has earned their trust and their loyalty.

A princess of the king they honor so much is just like encountering the real thing. They and their land are the answer to your safety. And we must get you as far away as possible from the palace." Satuu answered, assuring Debace.

"Anger an Altura and it may as well be the last thing you do," Satuu's words echoed in Debace's head. "That didn't help much." She whined quietly.

Debace looked behind them. For the last couple of nights, since they had left Beatrix, her dreams were haunted not only by her parents and Sou Harra, but also by Beatrix and her final breaths of life.

She had decided long ago that Sou Harra was a monster but didn't dwell on it much until now, and her hatred only grew more and more. Now, she had made a pact with herself. Either she kills Sou Harra, or she dies trying.

Satuu soon slowed to a stop as the sun rose higher and higher into the sky. "We should eat." He explained when Debace gave him a questioning glance as she hopped off his back.

Debace stood beside Satuu and quickly got the saddle bag. She pulled out some dried meat for herself and some apples for her and Satuu to share.

Debace handed Satuu an apple. She began to take a bite out of an apple but decided otherwise when thoughts of Beatrix popped into her head. "Did we really have to leave her," Debace thought.

She pondered on whether she should talk to Satuu and decided to ask. "Satuu, why did we leave Beatrix? Sou Harra is a monster and we both know that, why did we leave her and her mother to their deaths?"

Debace let a few tears roll down her cheek. "What if that was me," she thought.

"We had no choice, Debace. I cannot risk your life for anyone. Not even one I love." Satuu replied and laid his head down, trying to avoid questioning. He had wondered why they had left them, himself.

Debace bit into a piece of jerky and lay, basking in the sun. She stared at the sky and pictured her and her parents playing in the fields again. "I love you," she thought, "I love you so much."

When Debace and Satuu had eaten their fill, they packed up and rode further toward the land of the Alturas.

"Satuu, do you think that the Alturas will..." Debace had to swallow hard before she continued, "attack us?" she looked down at Satuu as if to look him in the eye but knew she couldn't, for it was impossible from his back.

"There is a possibility, but it is highly unlikely. I have fought at your father's side since before he even became Emperor and many recognize me as a friend of the Empire. Of course, there always is you." Satuu replied.

Lines of worry appeared on Debace's forehead. "Why me?" she asked.

"Because, you are the princess and your influence on this kingdom is well-known. Many know your face or at least know about the child that saved her mother." Satuu replied, not even able to catch himself before he said too much information.

"Saved my mother? What do you mean?" Debace began to think of the conversation that she had heard between Satuu and Beatrix.

"You will know soon enough, my child." Satuu said, trying to avoid the truth that shouldn't be known to this young child.

Debace, sensing the tension in Satuu, dropped the subject. No matter how much she questioned, Satuu wouldn't reveal very much. Satuu was too guarded to let it slip because of a 5 year olds questions.

She slumped over to rest her tired back from the position of a young lady on the back of a horse and closed her eyes. "Confusion, all I know is confusion," she thought.

Debace rolled her head around to relieve the tension in her neck that seemed to be a constant pain now. She picked up her head and straightened her back before opening her eyes once more.

"Satuu? What is that?" Debace asked as she pointed her finger at a dot in the distance.

Satuu quickened his pace and threw his head up in enthusiasm. "That, my child, is the Alturas land."

Chapter 8

Satuu slowed his pace as the feeling of anxiety boiled up inside him. An emotion brushed through his thoughts, one of evil and deceit. He walked slowly, closer and closer as he realized the cause of this dangerous feeling.

"What happened?" Debace asked as she looked upon the cold, dead faces. Every where she looked, from the waters to the middle of this small settlement, those same cold, dead faces stared back at her, giving her chills.

"I don't know." Satuu said cautiously.

He slowly walked among the corpses and searched for any sign of life. Thousands of despaired bodies lay strewn across the land.

Debace buried her head in Satuu's neck. She couldn't bear to see the faces of the poor beings that died because of her.

"They didn't die because of you, Debace." Satuu said, hearing her thoughts. Debace gasped but was in too much agony to question.

She grabbed Satuu's mane and hugged against his neck. "Why else would so many die, when someone evil is chasing us?" Debace asked.

Suddenly, a scream of agony reached Debace's ears. She screamed in return, a crawly feeling enveloping her.

Finally recovering herself, she jumped off Satuu's back and ran towards the source.

"Debace, get back here!" Sattu called after her, but Debace was already running through the dead Alturas to the one in so much pain.

Finally, she reached a child that looked about her age. "Run! Run away!" The child begged for her to leave, tears rolling down her rough cheeks, but Debace couldn't just leave.

She pushed the plea from her mind and looked over the injuries. The child had some minor bruises and a large gash in her stomach. Debace dropped to her knees beside the helpless Altura.

Tears began to push against her eyelids but she refused to relieve the tears that had not yet fallen. She had to be strong.

She stroked the Altura's head and cooed softly to calm her. The Altura relaxed and laid her head on Debace's lap. She closed her eyes and let the last bit of life in her disappear in peace.

Debace lay there with the child that could have just as easily been her, dead on another's lap. She let tears slide down her face, mourning the terrible death of these poor creatures.

She suddenly felt a soft muzzle on her face, comforting her. "Satuu, how could anyone do this? Evil or not, this is just..." she gasped as she looked up not to Satuu, but to a beautiful mare, its eyes just as comforting as its soft muzzle.

Debace sat there, entranced in those beautiful, black eyes. In them, she saw protection and comfort, love and compassion, but most of all, she saw, to her surprise, her mother. Who was this horse?

She retreated in fear as she heard voices and a terrible, cackling laugh. She looked towards where the laugh came from and saw that same terrible face. "Sou Harra," she glowered. She looked back towards where the black horse had been but only saw the waters of the Azorean sea.

"Debace, come." She heard a familiar voice from somewhere behind her. She turned around and saw Satuu, eyes pleading her to quickly follow him. She nodded in understanding and began to get up.

"Ah, you thought you could hide?" a fearsome voice announced towards Debace. She looked to see who had spoken and saw Sou

Harra glaring right at her. Satuu protectively blocked her sight of Sou Harra.

Debace felt anger begin to boil up inside her, blocking all fear she had once felt. She saw her mother's face and the child she had just one moment ago comforted, and then the black mare. Something about that mare reminded her of her mother.

But how could it be? She had come to believe her mother was dead, end of story. "There was one possibility. But that was impossible," Debace thought. That had been mere myth, part of her bedtime stories. That was what her father had told her. It was just impossible.

"Debace run! Now," she was wrenched from her thoughts by Satuu's command. She looked at him to confirm what she had heard ring in her mind. He nodded and turned toward Sou Harra.

She turned away and ran as fast as her legs would take her, away from the monster who prayed for her death.

Sou Harra laughed. "You think you will be able to protect her? She will die, with or without your help." Sou Harra screamed.

Debace stopped to look behind her and saw that same elegant herd of horses, rowed behind Satuu, and, in the back, that same beautiful, black mare.

"Debace run. Don't stop or look behind you, just run!" She heard Satuu's voice ring in her head once more.

Debace looked around in confusion. She wanted to obey Satuu but couldn't leave him alone. She felt her anger boil up inside her and a tingling feeling at the tips of her fingers.

She closed her eyes and pictured her mother and father, how distraught they looked, and all of the poor souls that suffered at the hands of this monster.

Her eyes flew open and words began to flow from her mouth. Words she did not know but suddenly spoke, "Wenrija Goje Me Pesijo Olosja Pento eh!" She raised her hands, supporting a large ball of glowing energy and threw it toward Sou Harra without hesitation.

It hit its target before Sou Harra could say a counter spell. He lay there still on the ground, stunned for the moment.

"Satuu, come on. Let's get out of here." She yelled as Satuu and the herd of wild horses ran towards her. She jumped onto Satuu's back and landed perfectly. She rejoiced throwing her hands up in the air.

Suddenly, she felt dizzy and felt herself falling off Satuu's back. The last thing she remembered was thinking of a safe place and imagining being in what seemed to be the oblivion and then landing on a soft ground. Or, had she imagined it.

Chapter 9

Debace rose, gasping for breath. She reached up her hand to her throat and scratched at it as if to grab the cause of her shortened breaths. She fell back on the hard, cold ground beneath her and lay silently, slowly catching her breath.

Life seemed to slip away from her as she lay and tried to recollect the recent events. Her memories were black and she suddenly noticed her eyesight was as well. She opened her eyes but quickly closed them as a reflex to the sudden brightness.

Her head throbbed and she tried not to cry because of the pain. She gritted her teeth and tried to rise to her feet.

When she finally stood somewhat straight, her knees buckled in pain and she fell to the stone floor.

"Stone? Where am I," Debace thought as she looked around, her eyes barely open and still adjusting to the light.

Finally, she opened her eyes wide in surprise as she realized where she was. "*When wild horses still roamed this earth freely, there was a cave that a beautiful horse claimed. This cave proved to be a sanctuary and saved the life of this one horse. But it also was said to be the undoing of that horse's human form, eternally locking it in a horse's body.*" Her mother's story suddenly popped into her head.

She had always told her that story before she went to bed and remembered asking, "Who was that horse? Will I ever see her?" She looked around the cave, noticing every detail that fit the description that her mother had given her.

She remembered everything her mother had told her about this cave. It was her favorite story and she always dreamed that she would be in that very cave, and that that cave would be <u>her</u> sanctuary. Now it seemed that this dream had come true.

For once, there was no pain and suffering, no cries, and no unwanted visitors. How long had it been since she had been safely in bed? "A long time, too long of a time,"

She chanced standing again and this time wasn't welcomed by the jeering pain in her knees. She took a few steps and rested on a stone.

She looked around, expecting to see Satuu there to comfort her but only saw a deep darkness. She suddenly felt alone and began to sob for someone to comfort her. She wouldn't even mind one of those Alturas.

"Alturas," she thought in terror. Her mind filled with details of the past few weeks and she began to get dizzy. Thankful for the stone for support, she sat down and slowly dozed off, leaning against the stone.

Those many terrible memories just proved to be too much for her.

Debace's dreams were haunted by her past.

In one dream, Debace was running into the barn, ready for her daily ride, when her father grabbed her just before entering the large wooden doors. That was when she first saw Satuu. She remembered the horrified look on Father's face and didn't know what to make of it. She became scared and wished she was back in the Ahab with mother.

She closed her eyes and when she opened them, she was with her mother. She giggled and ran around her, peeking around her mother's figure, looking up at her beautiful smile.

Suddenly her dreams lurched from her mother's smiling face to when Sou Harra's men had her in a terrified state of mind. No matter how Debace tried she couldn't get herself off the saddle and her legs felt like bags of sand. She looked down at Satuu and tried to yell at him for not stopping but her voice was mute.

All of a sudden, Debace wasn't riding on the back of a horse but falling into the black oblivion. Her limbs flapped and no matter how hard she tried, she couldn't wake up.

She screamed as she saw the bottom coming closer and then found herself alone in a desert.

She quickly stood and brushed sand from her tunic. She looked around and saw a short, skeletal man walk towards her. She yelled at him in anger, not knowing why, but her voice was lost in the howling wind.

The man held out his hand and boomed, "It is time!" Debace felt the ground pitch from underneath her and found herself careening into a black hole.

Debace rose from her spot on the cold floor and screamed in fear. Her eyes were wide open in shock and she looked around to make sure that she wasn't just in another one of her terrible nightmares.

She tried to recollect herself and remembered where she was. She looked around for something to ease the feeling of discomfort and loneliness that suddenly filled her and saw a dark figure in the shadows.

She shied away in fear, envisioning that terrible man that had thrown her into the black hole that had so suddenly awoken her. She looked closer and saw the figure move towards her, slowly and cautiously. She heard a soft whinny and a beautiful black mare appeared in the dim light.

Debace thought of the Wild Horse that had once had this cave as its own, her mother's voice echoing in her head.

"A cave, not this one," she tried to reason but the resemblance was unnatural.

Debace felt a tugging at the edge of her mind, the kind of tug when Satuu wished to speak respectively. She welcomed it, enjoying something familiar. "Child, how did you get here?" A voice echoed in her head.

She gasped at the sound of what she thought to be her mother's voice. She didn't answer the question but merely stared in awe at this magnificent creature.

"You are too young to have achieved what would be the only way to this place. Satuu is worried sick." This time Debace thought hard on the conversation and recognized Satuu's name.

"Where am I?" she managed to say past her parched lips. The mare didn't answer but signaled for Debace to follow her. Debace obeyed and found herself in front of a pool of water. She dropped to her knees and drank greedily.

When she finished, she looked at the mare expectantly, wanting to know her previous question. "Soranthian cave, my child," the mare answered lying down on the soft grass beside the stream.

Debace looked into the stream at her own reflection. She was tall for her young age of 5, her long, dark brown hair matted with sweat and mud. She looked over and saw the mare staring at her in confusion.

In response, Debace asked, "Who are you? How did I get here? Where is Satuu?" She was bound to get the answer of at least one question.

The mare's eye twinkled with remembering and she looked down in the stream. "Those of my herd call me Gloriensa, which means 'lost mother'. I truly don't know how you got here. I am the only known living creature of the outside world that can come here as I please, but I do know where Satuu is."

Debace waited a moment to let the information register. "Is he ok?" Debace asked, afraid of the answer.

Gloriensa waited to answer. "Satuu was captured and taken back to the Empire. From my information, the trip was hard on him but he managed to escape with the help of my brethren. But he sent a message for you." Gloriensa waited for Debace to look at her, tears rolling down her face.

"It's my fault. What will I do now?" She pleaded.

"It is not your fault. Don't worry about him; he can take care of himself. But you must go on your journey without him," Gloriensa stood and walked back towards the cave.

"Without Satuu, that would be a living nightmare," Debace thought. She felt as though she had just begun her long journey and wished it away. Her family was gone and now she had to travel on alone. What else was there for her?

Debace stood and walked to the cave, her limbs heavy with fatigue.

When she finally reached the entrance, Gloriensa stopped her in her tracks. "Satuu sent a message that shouldn't be delayed. You proved yourself strong and opened an option of travel. But I warn you, this option is dangerous for someone of your age. You may lose much of what you may not be able to get back. Are you willing?" Debace stepped back in surprise. What else did Satuu have in mind that was so dangerous?

She began to feel afraid but soon decided that anything that Satuu had in mind was the best. She shook her head and slowly followed Gloriensa. She felt her head droop and she wished for a bed and her mother to sing her to sleep.

"You must leave at once! Hurry, this is the only time you can. If you don't leave now, all will be lost to evil and suffering." Debace was wrenched from her thoughts and she stumbled into Gloriensa. Why was she being so urgent all of a sudden?

Her knees began to ache and she felt dizzy, but felt a force stronger than her fatigue pulling at her. She saw her nightmare of the figure and screamed as he repeated his final words.

"Why?" she asked Gloriensa as she fell into the dark oblivion.

Her breaths were shortened and she felt as though her lungs were ripping out of her chest. She felt a sharp pain in her head and saw a familiar scene from many of her dreams. A herd of horses, dazzling at the sight but she knew how deadly they could be. They were the Wild Horses. As she felt her conscience fall away she thought of her mother and readied herself for the death she thought she deserved. But matters were much different.

She landed hard on the ground that surely shattered every bone in her body. Her life faded and she saw a light beckoning her to follow. She closed her eyes and let peace flood her.

Chapter 10

Jonathan ran out of his house. Something wasn't right and that loud bang wasn't just gunfire. He ran towards the barn and looked inside to find nothing but dust mites. "Hello? Is someone there?" he asked. No reply.

He slowly walked out towards the pasture and noticed Kendra running to him, frantically waving her arms. "Jonathan! There is a child. A child has fallen from the sky!"

Jonathan doubted the sanity of Kendra's words. "A child fall from the sky," he thought, "impossible." Nonetheless, he succumbed to her urging and shoving, and followed her to her home just up the path.

"Jonathan, I think she is really hurt. She fell with a blow that no one could survive and she looks fairly young. Come, quickly." Kendra urged Jonathan to quicken his pace. Jonathan smiled to himself at Kendra's skeptics.

She was usually the calm warrior but when it came to children, she had a very soft heart. "Which would be understandable, but maybe too soft," Jonathan thought.

They ran past the stream and towards a huge oak tree. He looked up at the house located on its high, sturdy limbs, Kendra's home.

He never understood why she didn't just have her house on the ground like normal people but she always said that she kept secrets up there. At the time he had taken that statement as a joke but pondered on the unusual possibility.

Finally, Kendra and Jonathan reached a wide open valley, hay colored grasses growing in all directions and a small dot in the distance, unsettling the grass stalks. Jonathan began to become puzzled as they neared the object and it took on a small human form.

When they finally were at the object's side Jonathan realized that this was a *real* child, a living breathing being that was terribly hurt.

Jonathan lowered his hand to the child's chest and let a golden glow flow from his finger tips into the child. "Her heart rate is much too low, and she has broken several ribs. It looks like she has some major internal bleeding, also." He said as his eyes glazed with magic, visioning the child's inner parts.

"Can you help her?" Kendra asked, her eyes pleading. Jonathan closed his eyes and thought of a powerful healer, the wounds were just too much for him to treat. He needed Derrick.

"Derrick, do you know who he is? Kendra, we need Derrick. These wounds are too bad for me to heal alone. Hurry, she won't live long. I will carry her to my home, meet us there with Derrick. Now, GO!" Jonathan ordered. Kendra gracefully jumped to her feet and ran with the speed of light.

Jonathan looked back down at the small child. Who was this girl, falling out of the sky? He studied her for a moment before carefully picking her up and carrying her to his house.

She had long dark brown hair, matted down as though she had been through many nights without so much as a swim. Her face was pale at the moment and her lips parched. Her hands felt clammy when he gathered her up.

He quickly carried her down the dirt path and set her on a hand sown sofa, filled with sheep's wool, making it feel soft and plushy. He carried in some water and a blanket and poured the water on her mouth. She groaned and tried to flip but decided against it.

"This child has been through a lot," he thought. He raised his hands and blue sparks flew onto the numerous cuts and scrapes that covered her arms and legs. She had a large bruise on her head and it was swelling terribly. "Concussion," Jonathan thought as he draped the blanket over her.

Debace felt light engulf her, closing her eyes quickly and welcoming the darkness that invited her. She heard a scream and a sharp pain went through her side. She felt her conscience slip and the pain overwhelmed her curiosity of where she may be. Her head pounded with the failing beats of her heart and suddenly, she went numb.

"This is it," she thought, "I'll see you soon Mother."

When Kendra got to Jonathan's house with Derrick, Jonathan thought it was too late. "She has a terrible fever and that concussion on her head could have killed her by its self. I truly don't know how she is still alive." Derrick informed him.

His sad and amazed eyes locked on the small child. "She has been through too much for such a young one," he thought. He held his hand over her forehead and bright sparks alighted from his palm. The swelling ceased for a moment, and she laid still, her fever stunned.

"Isn't there something we can do for her? I mean, she's so young!" Kendra asked passionately "No child should die so young." She mumbled, mostly to herself than anyone else.

Jonathan looked up at her, seeing her eyes well up with tears. "Kendra, why don't you go to the kitchen? Fix some tea." Jonathan offered. Kendra nodded her head and slowly walked to the small kitchen.

Jonathan watched her go and wished there was something he could do to ease her pain, knowing the memories of her son were haunting her unmercifully. He knew how terrible it felt to lose someone very close to you and not know why.

"Jonathan, come with me. We need to talk." Derrick ordered.

He walked outside and waited in the doorway for Jonathan to catch up with him. When he did, Derrick immediately began walking. They walked in silence up into the pasture that belonged to Jonathan when Derrick began to speak. "Jonathan, there is something about that child that we don't understand. No child of that age could have survived what she has. It is simply impossible. Cohilla himself would have barely survived. And the fact that she is a small child with this ability, well it just troubles me."

Derrick's troubled eyes trailed the ground. Jonathan looked around to find something to distract himself from the uneasy position that he had just been put in. He, too, was troubled by the unusual child that seemed to just have fallen out of the sky. But what was more troubling was the thought that she could actually survive. Suddenly, Jonathan heard something.

Jonathan stopped walking. Something was in the bushes, something very large. He swirled around to see a beautiful white stallion standing between two trees. "All is well, Debace will live. Keep her until the time is right," Jonathan heard a strange voice echo through his head. Jonathan gasped in surprise and started toward the stallion. "Go and see for yourself," and with that last word, the stallion galloped off into the horizon, whipping by Jonathan.

He watched as the magnificent creature joined a large herd at the top of the hill, and they all galloped off into the distance.

"Jonathan! Come look!" Jonathan jumped at the sound of Kendra's voice.

"It can't be," Jonathan thought as he thought back on what the stallion had said to him. He started at a sprint towards the house, leaving Derrick behind.

When Jonathan reached the house, he burst through the door and ran to the child. "Where is my mother? Is Satuu here, too? Am I dead? Is father ok?" she was blabbering on, eyes still glazed with fever. Jonathan grabbed a damp cloth and dabbed her forehead with it.

Suddenly a question popped up that stunned Jonathan, "Who am I?" He looked at the child with sadness. Her experiences were gone. Everything she may have been was now never to be known. He thought of the stallion and the name that he had said, *Debace.* It was a beautiful name and sounded so familiar. "Debace." He said, before he could catch himself.

Debace woke to a woman crying. "Mother?" she whispered. The woman quickly got up and ran to her side. Her tearstained face was nothing like mother's face. "Who are you? Where am..."

Suddenly, Debace fell silent. "Debace, go now in peace, live life, and grow strong," She heard a familiar voice ring in her head.

"Satuu?" she whispered, trying to pick up her head to see her friend, but her efforts were only rewarded with failure.

She watched helplessly as the woman ran outside and a tall man suddenly appeared in the doorway. She started to ask what happened and suddenly her head went blank. Everything, as if her mind had been wiped clean. She felt very unsettled and asked the man, "Who am I?"

He seemed to think on something and she saw him open his mouth, "Debace." Nothing familiar about the name struck her. She saw the sad expression on his face and tears well up in his eyes. She closed her eyes, not realizing how tired she felt until just that moment, and soon fell into a peaceful sleep.

Chapter 11

*D*ebace slowly opened her eyes. Her eyelids felt like sacks of sand and she felt limp all over.

She lay still and stared up at the plaster ceiling, contemplating on questions that bounced in her head. Where am I? What happened? Who am I? How did I get here? She tried to raise her head but felt every muscle and tissue in her body jolt with pain. She groaned in agony.

Suddenly, a tall man appeared at her side. He stroked her scalp caringly and cooed to her softly. He grabbed a damp rag and dabbed it on her forehead.

Debace studied his appearance in awe. He had shockingly blue eyes, slightly dirty blonde hair, and prominent facial features. He had wide set shoulders and muscular arms that revealed hard work. His face seemed to carry a burden of sadness when he looked upon her. "Who was this man?" She wondered.

One word rang through her mind, a sort of gut feeling. "Father?" she repeated from her thoughts.

She watched as his expression grew into a grief stricken sadness and she saw a small tear roll down his cheek.

She raised her hand weakly and wiped away the tear. She looked at him pleadingly. "Father?" she asked again, desperation clear in her voice.

He seemed to contemplate on the answer and hesitated only a moment. "Yes, you are safe now. Father is here." He replied, as he stroked her hair carefully and caringly.

Debace turned her head to look up at the plastered ceiling. "This is my home. I am home," she thought as she closed her eyes and fell asleep.

Debace was standing in the middle of a field. Her head reeling with all kinds of warnings, warnings that said she shouldn't be here.

She looked up at the sound of footsteps, watching a dazzling white stallion walking toward her. Debace stepped back a pace and looked wide-eyed as a herd of beautiful horses came from behind the stallion. "Who... who are you?" she stammered.

She felt a tug at the edge of her mind and suddenly a voice rang in her thoughts, "Debace, you are safe. Answers will come soon, yet now is too early. Now, sleep."

Debace felt a sudden breeze and lay on the soft ground. She slowly closed her eyes; the last thing she saw was a black mare gallop her way and lay beside her lovingly.

Debace woke with a start. She tried to sit up but once again was restrained by the straps that held her still. She let out a long sigh, attracting attention to her as she desperately pulled at the restraints. "Let me out! I must get out of here." She screamed as a woman appeared at her side. "Let me go!" she yelled.

Suddenly a man stood above her. Debace's eyes went wide open as she recognized him from one of her memories. "Father, help me." She pleaded. The man kneeled down and pulled at the restraints. Finally, they loosened and Debace sat up slowly.

When she finally was on her feet, she looked around the small house. The walls were plastered the same as the ceiling. There was a doorway that led to a kitchen and beside it, shelves that held cooking utensils. There weren't many decorations in the house except the occasional picture or painting.

She looked at the small table that was next to the cot she had slept on. On top of it was a small vase of daffodils and snapdragons. She watched closely as one of the snapdragons opened its petals and snipped off a dead flower.

Debace looked at the man she called father and asked, "Who am I?" She had a mild recollection of one name that sounded too beautiful to speak.

"Debace." The man replied.

"Jonathan?" The woman laid a hand on his shoulder and questioned.

"Stay here Debace. I will be back." He replied as he and the woman walked into the kitchen. Debace nodded and sat on the cot.

"Jonathan, what is going on? Why is she calling you 'father'?" Kendra asked, reaching out her hand to grasp his in hers.

Jonathan waited a moment before responding. "It breaks my heart that she has lost everything. Even her recollection of it is gone. It would have broken my heart even more if I had to tell her that the one person she calls for is probably dead or will never find her. I couldn't do that to her." Jonathan replied, slightly raising his voice.

Kendra raised her hand to his cheek. She looked worriedly into his eyes, seeing old pain. She had been through it also. She knew the pain he had endured long ago. Just as he did, she had lost loved ones to a slaughter.

She squeezed his hand slightly and lightly kissed him on the cheek. "Do what you must. But, remember, she'll have to know some day." Kendra walked out of the kitchen and went to Debace.

Jonathan raised his hand to where Kendra's lips had been. Once again he reminded himself that he was connected to another, a sort of bond. And that other was gone forever. And with her she took any chance of him moving on.

Debace looked up as the woman walked towards her. She studied her for a long moment, taking in every detail. She was tall, yet not as tall as Jonathan. Her sleek blonde hair shone in the light of the house. She had emerald green eyes and a full figure.

The woman motioned for Debace to move over to make room for her. "My name is Kendra. Are you comfortable?" the woman gestured with her hand towards Debace. Debace nodded, awe struck by how friendly this woman seemed to be.

"I'm Deb... Debace." Debace said, still struggling to say the name that she had been given. "Kendra, where is this place?" Debace probed, but she didn't know that her thoughts were heard.

Kendra's eyes flew open in surprise, and then she settled into a comfortable position, facing Debace, as if she had a long story to tell. "You are in Trencha. This land is the end of this continent. If you continue in the Sulonta sea, you will find yourself on the island of Pentos, or the realm of the night. Would you like a drink, dear?" Kendra asked, rising to her feet. Debace nodded and Kendra walked to the kitchen.

Jonathan was still in the same place where Kendra had left him. Kendra walked passed him and grabbed a glass. "What is so wrong? Why is it that I feel like the strong one right now when usually you are the one with the emotions of steal? Talk to me." Kendra pleaded, setting the glass down.

"Something about that girl reminds me of Tori. Maybe I just need some rest. You know, I haven't slept since she has been here." And with that, Jonathan walked to his room and lay down, falling into a gentle slumber.

Kendra thought back to when Debace seemed to have reached into her mind. She remembered how Deinte had done just that and how Jonathan had always complained about how Tory, his first and last child, had always probed his mind.

Kendra felt tears rush forward as she thought of her and Deinte's young child, Griffen. Each had had a sort of attitude or knowledge, and all had been slaughtered by the army of Sou Harra.

She pushed the thought away and steadied herself, slowly getting her emotions under control. She grabbed the glass of water and brought it to Debace.

"Father, where are you going?" Debace asked as Jonathan walked through the living room and into his bedroom.

"No where, Debace. I am just going to take a nap." He answered briskly. Debace felt a longing to follow him but sensed by his tense answer that he needed some time to himself.

Kendra appeared in the doorway, a troubled look upon her face.

"What's wrong?" Debace asked as Kendra handed her the drink.

Kendra tried to think but didn't exactly know what was wrong, or at least where to begin. "How did you do that?" Kendra asked.

Debace gave a confused look, "What?"

"When you, well you know, kind of spoke with your mind." Kendra struggled to find the right words.

Debace took a sip of the water. It slowly slid down her throat, relieving her parched insides. Suddenly she seemed to ponder the question and shook her head in dismay. "I really don't know. I can't remember anything." She took another sip of water absentmindedly. "Can't everyone do it?" Debace asked, assuming that it was just unusual for her age.

"What is my age?" Debace thought. Debace stood and walked to a small mirror.

"No, rarely will you find another… person who can do what you did." Kendra said, struggling to find the right word to describe one of such power.

Debace barely listened to Kendra. She was too busy looking at herself, trying to find some kind of answer. She ran her fingers through her long, slightly dark brown hair. Her eyes were a sort of caramel, slightly lighter, and were surrounded by long dark eyelashes. "Kendra, how long have you known me?" Debace asked, hoping to know something to fill the void that filled her head.

Kendra got up from her spot on the cot and walked to Debace's side. "Sadly, child, I barely know you." Debace looked up at Kendra with a confused look.

Kendra thought about what Jonathan had said, 'Something about that girl reminds me of Tori.' She could see now, why he was so upset about the resemblance. They both had those small glints in their eyes, a sort of signal that they had a secret, and the same unusual ability to turn you inside out with just one look. The thought twisted Kendra's stomach.

"Kendra, are you my mother?" she asked in a voice barely audible.

Kendra was instantly moved by the question. She thought about another chance to be a mother, to care for a child. She leaned down and whispered in her ear, "If you want me to be, I can be." Kendra said, walking over to the cot.

Debace grinned and followed her, sitting next to her and leaning on her shoulder. Silence washed over the house as all succumbed to their body's need of rest.

Debace woke with a start, feeling a rough hand against her forehead. She opened her eyes and jumped when she saw the rugged face of the village medical magician, Derrick.

"The fever is gone, her bones are healed, and the concussion seems to have just disappeared. I have checked her over also, NO other magic helped this miraculous heal, except the occasional pain killer. She is fully recovered as of today." He announced.

Debace glanced up and realized that Jonathan was standing above her. She instantly relaxed and lay back, comprehending this doctor's words. "Fully recovered," she thought happily as she drifted into a peaceful slumber.

Chapter 12

When Debace awoke again, the sun had just passed mid-rise. She slowly stood, her knees still feeling slightly wobbly, and looked about her.

She saw light shining through a small window next to the door and a small fan blowing lightly inside the house. Debace walked over to examine the fan and noticed that nothing powered it.

She reached her hand toward the back and felt slight pressure. When she looked behind the fan, she saw a small sphere of glowing energy. Debace tried to run her hand through the sphere but her actions were only rewarded by a sharp shock, first beginning at her fingers and proceeding up her arm. She quickly withdrew her hand and her arm proceeded to be numb, only for a quick moment, before disappearing all together.

"I see you have taken it upon yourself to, well, by what my mother used to say, learn from experiences. Are you hungry?"

Debace jumped at the sound of Jonathan's voice. She turned quickly to face him and smiled brightly. "What is this?" She asked pointing at the sphere that had just shocked her.

Jonathan walked over to Debace's side. He pointed to the glowing sphere behind the fan and asked, "This? That is what powers this fan.

Some call it magic, but personally, I think that is too immature. It can also be verified as Energy or dynamism. You see the glowing parts and streaks?" Jonathan pointed to the long streak of light emanating from the sphere, "Those are caused by the continued movement of this energy. That shock you got is the result of continued movement as well."

Debace looked down at her feet as she blushed by her foolishness. "But, how is it made?" Debace asked, changing the subject.

"I made them. There are certain energy pockets in our systems which we can summon for small activities. Some are more powerful than others but it just depends on their line of descent. For example, your doctor is from a long line of practiced medical magicians. Therefore he could do more help to a person in need than I." Jonathan put his arm around Debace and guided her toward the kitchen. "Come, Debace, you need to eat. Would you like some orange juice?" Jonathan asked.

Debace nodded and sat down at the table. She watched as Jonathan poured a glass of orange juice and set it on the table in front of her. "Who was that man? You know the one that said 'Fully recovered'." She asked.

Jonathan looked up and seemed to contemplate his answer. "You remember what I said about your doctor? Well, his name is Derrick; he is the most professional medical magician I have ever seen. I don't know what I would've done without him. He sa…" Jonathan stopped quickly and glanced at Debace to make sure that she hadn't caught his intentions. "She's too young. I just can't," he thought.

Debace saw the silence as an excuse to leave. She stood and walked to his side. "Where's Kendra?" she asked.

Jonathan looked down at Debace. "She's down the road. I will walk you." Jonathan said, grabbing his hat from a hook protruding from the wall.

Debace backed away when he tried to guide her to the door. "Can I walk myself? I'd like to see what's around." Debace asked. Jonathan hesitated, not wanting her to walk alone. "Let me walk, please. I will be fine, Father," Jonathan heard a very convincing voice echo in his head.

He turned his head towards Debace in shock, uttering one word, "Tori?" Debace looked questioningly at Jonathan.

Suddenly she uttered words that seemed to be from someone else. She didn't know what was going on, just watched the expressions on Jonathan's face as she spoke, "La Quinta Es p'ista. Ret'san pouto."

Jonathan's mouth gaped open. He heard something that he had thought died long ago. Yet, now in this small child was the past that cut deeply in his emotions. He grasped Debace's shoulders, begging an explanation. "Do you know what you just said? Debace, tell me; what did you say?"

Debace gave a questioning glance at Jonathan. She thought hard, trying to find the explanation he so desperately needed. "I really don't know. Are you ok?" Debace softly touched Jonathan's arm, seeing his distant look.

Jonathan looked down at Debace, seeing Tory for a moment. "I can't do this," Jonathan thought. His feelings were fighting each other deep inside for the conquering. His heart was battling with his past, trying to make sense of his feelings. The words that Debace had just said struck like a spear. He saw Tory, her eyes distant as she died, saying something, a confession. "Debace, go get dressed. I'll take you to Kendra."

Jonathan sat down in order to clear his mind. "Could Debace be the one? Where did she come from? How did she say that," questions weaved their ways as burdens would have through his mind, and finally to his heart. "It can't be," Jonathan reasoned as Debace walked out of the room with a leather tunic on. Her hair was tied up in a thong and she seemed to be ready to travel a great distance.

Jonathan smiled, wrapping his arm around Debace. As they walked out the door, Jonathan reasoned once again, "She can't be," then, he led Debace to a path leading into the woods.

Chapter 13

Debace looked up at Jonathan worriedly as they entered the dark trees. Jonathan looked down at Debace and smiled, assuring her. "It's ok, Debace. These areas are protected."

They stared at each other for quite some time. Debace broke their gaze and looked ahead of her. The dark seemed to envelope her as they went deeper and deeper. She felt like the trees were moving closer, trying to suffocate her.

She stopped and took a deep breath, not realizing she had been holding it. She felt a hot, clammy feeling seem to wash over her. Her vision began to come in spurts, small black spots covering it like a checker board. Her legs felt weak, like they would give out at any moment. She let go of Jonathan's hand, stopping in her tracks.

Jonathan looked back at Debace and saw her sway. He ran to her side and let her fall into his arms. "Debace! Debace?"

Jonathan stroked her hairline and suddenly saw the color drain from Debace's face. He gasped and jumped up, Debace still in his arms. He ran through the trees with great speed, Debace's limp form reminding him to move fast. He finally reached the end of the trees and ran towards the large oak tree that held Kendra's home.

Debace felt cold, damp earth under her cheek. She bolted up right and looked about her. She listened for some sign of where she was nearby, but only heard the song of the inhabitants of this strange place.

Her heart beat faster as she heard a sound, disturbing the natural songs. She listened closer and realized that it was foot steps of some kind. She turned quickly and found a beautiful white stallion standing in front of her. "Who are you?" Debace asked, hearing her own voice as if it were of someone else's.

She saw the stallion move his ears back in confusion, then its mouth open. Debace leaned closer to hear what the stallion had to say but merely heard the soft noises of this forest.

Suddenly, the stallion turned its head out in the damp growth of the forest. Debace tried to ask what was wrong but her voice was lost to the sound of voices in the distance. "Voices?" Debace said aloud, looking in the direction of the unusual sounds.

She looked back at the stallion and saw that he was running. "Wait! Please, don't leave me alone!" she yelled but her voice was small and weak. She watched as he ran away, leaving her behind.

Suddenly, a rough hand grabbed her shoulder. She turned around slowly to view a sneer upon an evil face. She tried to scream but her voice seemed to have run with the stallion.

"Now I have you! You will die!" The man yelled as he drew a sword from his side. She closed her eyes, awaiting her death.

"Debace! Wake up, you must wake up!" Debace heard a familiar voice ring in her ear. She slowly opened her eyes and saw Jonathan's worried gaze.

"Father, what happened?" She asked in a weak voice. Jonathan laid a damp cloth on Debace's forehead. Her head felt swollen and for a moment she couldn't remember anything. Her eyelids felt heavy and she closed them.

She felt a light hand on her forehead and opened her eyes once again.

Suddenly, a flashback of her experience appeared before her eyes.

She heard the terrible choked voice of the man that had tried to kill her. She screamed and tried to retreat but a terrible pain rattled her tiny body. She clamped her teeth and fell to the ground.

Jonathan was by her side and softly whispering words of encouragement that it was ok and that there was nothing there. Debace squeezed her eyes shut to escape the horrible scene.

Tears flowed to her eyes and fell as she grasped Jonathan. "What is this?" she said in a low, terrified voice. Jonathan squeezed tighter.

"I don't know, Debace. It'll be alright." He said softly, trying to convince himself of this also. "What was happening?" He thought.

Here she was, screaming for mercy at an image that wasn't there. Something was terribly wrong and he would find out what it was.

Kendra ran into the room to see what was going on. "Is she ok?" she whispered in Jonathan's ear as he carefully rocked Debace.

Jonathan didn't answer but was lost in his own thoughts. He tried to think of someone who could answer all these questions but his mind was simply blank. Instead, he slowly rocked Debace to sleep, hoping everything would be alright.

Debace opened her eyes slowly, wondering what exactly had happened. Her head ached, as if she had fallen hard on it.

She sat up slowly and gazed about her. The home she was in was very foreign to her. The wooden walls separating each room, the animal skins that served as furniture, and as she glanced at the room she was in, she noticed a small painting.

She slowly stood and carefully walked towards the painting to closely observe it. It was one of a young woman, her hair flowing down over her shoulders. She had prominent facial features and a look of sadness that sent shivers down Debace's spine.

As Debace gazed into her soft brown eyes, she became lost in her own thoughts. She wondered who this woman was. Yet, try as she might, the woman struck no spark in her memory, merely a feel of familiarity. Debace turned her head side to side, trying to see the painting in every angle. "Who was this strange woman? Where did she come from?"

She reached out, her hand slowly tracing the lining of her face. She looked so familiar yet so alien. Confused, she turned around, gasping in surprise as she saw Kendra. "Oh hello," Debace exclaimed and bowed her head, embarrassed.

"Good morning, Debace. How did you sleep?" Kendra asked friendly, bringing her steaming glass to her lips.

"Ok. I had a nightmare, though." Debace admitted, remembering her dreams. She walked over to Kendra and wrapped her arms around her waist.

Kendra smiled as she wrapped her free hand around Debace, holding her close. She led Debace back to the couch she had slept on and sat her down. "Now," she said "tell me about this nightmare."

Debace squinted, remembering her horrid dream. "There was a man. One so hideous, he looked as if he walked dead. His hands were large but very skinny. Every bone in his body seemed to bulge. He carried a large staff of some kind, and it had this big crystal on top. He pointed at me and yelled with fury, 'It is time!' And then he was gone and suddenly everything was black and all I felt was pain, such great pain. Everything else just seemed to have dissolved away - smell, taste, sound. Everything," Debace stopped and took a deep breath. Her body shook just thinking of her dream. Why had she felt such pain? Had this truly happened or was it what she expected, just a dream? Why couldn't she REMEMBER?

Tears began to well up in her eyes and her voice began to crack as she went on to what she thought to be the worst part of all. "Then that dream had gone and another one appeared. I was in a woman's arms, laughing and giggling, trying to run free. It was sort of like it was a game. I remember her whispering in my ear how beautiful I would grow up to be. How strong my mind already was. I laughed like it was a joke. Then that picture dissolved and I was suddenly in a dark room. I was scared and I looked around the room. Suddenly I saw a bunch of people. I ran to them but they all went into a room. In the light I could only see one person, that same person in the last one. Her eyes were closed and she heaved every breath. I screamed something I do not recall. Someone grabbed me from behind and," Debace began wiping streams of tears from her face. She finally sniffed and continued. "and began to pull me away from the window. I began to speak something, I didn't understand it. But before I could finish the woman opened her eyes and spoke, 'La Quinta Es p'ista. Ret'san pouto.' And for some reason I understood, knowing that it must be done. I let the person drag me away, only saying one word."

Debace swallowed hard and looked Kendra in the eye. She wondered what Kendra thought of all this. "Grandmother. I called her grandmother."

Kendra hugged Debace tight, letting her cry into her tunic. She understood why this meant so much to her but still didn't quite understand. "Debace, was that why you looked so scared when I walked through the door, because of the nightmare?" Kendra asked.

Debace shook her head and she pointed her finger towards the painting she had been observing. "That's the woman, Kendra. She is the one from my dream." Debace watched Kendra's face as it drained of color. Now it was Kendra's turn to be afraid, for the woman on the wall was the dead Empress.

Chapter 14

Kendra's brow wrinkled in confusion as she gazed from Debace to the painting of the old Empress. Suddenly, she noticed that her mouth was gaping open and she closed it quickly, standing up and running her hand through Debace's hair. "I'll be right back." She said, slowly.

She gazed at the small girl, then turned and walked away trying not to seem too tense. She looked around at Debace one last time before slowly walking into the kitchen.

She kept walking until she was sure that she was out of sight and then grabbed the wall to steady herself, because her body shook from fear. "What did this mean," She thought to herself over and over. "Should I be worried?"

She contemplated this for quite some time, but shook herself from her thoughts when she heard Debace moving around and yelling, "Father!"

She slowly walked into the small room where she saw Debace and Jonathan embraced in a hug. Jonathan looked up at Kendra and smiled at her but his smile faded when he saw the expression on her face. Kendra gave a short nod of her head and walked back into the kitchen.

Jonathan squeezed Debace softly and whispered into her ear, "I'll be right back." Debace nodded, showing she understood and watched Jonathan walk into the kitchen after Kendra.

"What's the matter?" he asked after he was clear out of ear shot of Debace.

Kendra shuddered; she didn't know if she could even say it without screaming in fear. Yet, she gathered herself and began to speak, "Jonathan, what do we know about that girl?" she gazed at him as if he may tell her something she doesn't already know, yet he just looked back at her with a confused expression playing on his face. "Nothing, that's what! How do we know if she isn't of royal blood? Do you know the punishment for kidnapping royalty? DEATH!" she began to raise her voice and her eyes widened as she imagined them both being beheaded for a crime they had no idea they had committed.

"Kendra, what has brought you to this outrageous conclusion? Of course she's not of royal blood! If so she would have recognized that godforsaken painting you have on your wall." He smiled reassuringly.

Kendra grunted in frustration. "But that's it! She <u>did</u> recognize the painting! She told me about this nightmare that she had and told of how she had seen the Empress and called her *GRANDMOTHER!* Jonathan, we can't take that risk. You know how terrible it was when the royals came here! We live here in peace, now! And it will stay that way." She said lowering her head to look down at her hands in front of her.

Jonathan's mouth gaped open and anger played on his face. "You aren't suggesting that we throw her out to the world, and just watch as it engulfs her! You were the one who wanted to help her so bad and now that there are some minor complications you tuck your tail in and run! How can you be so heartless?"

He stared at her, never wavering until she answered shakily. "Jonathan, this could be the death of us. SHE could be the death of us! I don't wish to leave her alone but it may be necessary!" Tears streamed down her face as she saw the look of extreme disappointment in Jonathan's eyes.

He shook his head and said in a low voice after turning his back to her to walk away, "You may be able to just give up, but I cannot." And with saying this, walked back to Debace.

Chapter 15

*Y*ears passed by as Jonathan raised Debace as if she were his own. No one questioned how she came to be in his care, but some did marvel at the wondrous things that seemed to happen in her presence. Obstacles would suddenly disappear, the sick would find themselves cured, and all the while Debace stayed oblivious to the events happening around her. And Jonathan worked very hard to keep it that way.

Ever since that fateful day when she seemed to just fall out of the sky, he promised himself that he would never let anything happen to her. No matter what, he would protect her from anything.

Light poured into her room from the small window beside her head. Debace slowly opened her eyes, stretching to every corner of her small cot. She sat up and looked out the window at the field, green grass swaying in the wind and the sun slowly rising over the horizon. She marveled at how, every morning, this beautiful display of nature could take her breath away.

She sat there for quite a while, looking out on the horizon, still half expecting that same white horse from her dreams to appear and take her away, riding into the sunrise, bright beams of light rising into the sky. "Debace, breakfast is ready!" Debace jumped as her fathers voice rang through the house.

She jumped up, grabbed a loose tunic, and threw it on. "Coming!" she announced as she quickly brushed her long, dark hair and walked out of her room, into the living room, and then into the kitchen through the small doorway.

Debace walked in silently to find Jonathan sitting at the table, already eating his plate of eggs, bacon, and toast. She smiled and pulled out a chair to sit down.

Jonathan looked up and sighed. "How did you sleep?" he asked, leaning back in his chair.

"Good, but I had that dream again, Father! Only this time it felt different. I don't know how but it was different, lifelike even. First I'm on the back of a beautiful white stallion and it feels like we're riding as fast as the wind, then suddenly there's a whole herd of horses surrounding us. The sound of hooves hitting the hard ground increases until it is nearly unbearable and then suddenly it's quiet. I'm in a dark cave and confused. A black mare walks up and speaks to me. Yet all she said this time is 'The time has come'. It was so unusual, Father. After all this time why would my dream change?" She seemed to almost be pleading for the answer.

Her eyes were wide and adventurous, just waiting to see if he would know what she never did. "It's just a dream. That's all. Now eat your breakfast, today is going to be long." He told her, still watching her intently.

Debace abided to her father's wishes and began to eat her breakfast.

When both of them had finished, Debace got up and went to her room to get dressed. She grabbed a pair of pants and a tunic out of her small chest of drawers.

As she pulled off her sleep clothes she remembered her bruise on her hip from the day before. She touched it softly and thought about the day before.

She had been walking through the field when she heard the crying of an animal. She walked around trying to find the source until she finally found a small deer stuck in an animal trap, its leg stuck in the knot. She had slowly walked up to it, coaxing it and trying to get close enough to let it free when a large coyote had appeared out of the bushes.

The coyote growled loudly and bared its teeth at Debace as she stepped between the helpless creature and the coyote. She saw the coyote's ribs bulge beneath its mangy fur. The coyote lunged at Debace, and Debace ducked as the coyote flew over her. She ran to get between the coyote and the deer once again and the coyote lowered its body, the hair on its back standing straight up.

Debace looked around to find something to protect herself with and grabbed a large stick lying beside her. Once again, the coyote lunged at Debace and she swung the stick with all her might. Debace watched as the coyote quickly recovered from the blow and ran at her, full speed. Debace backed up a few paces, trying to ready herself for the blow but the coyote caught her by surprise.

She screamed in pain as she hit the tree beside her, her hand up to protect her face from the coyote's bared teeth. The coyote gave up on her and began to close in on the deer. Debace tried to get up to save it but the pain in her side was too great. She closed her eyes so she would not have to see the event before her.

Soon, she heard a growling in front of her and she quickly opened her eyes again. The whole pack had joined the stray coyote. Debace willed herself to get up but the pain in her side and fear paralyzed her.

Then, just as she thought that there was no hope, there was a flash of light and Debace heard yelping. Debace watched as the coyotes dispersed and a large white stallion appeard beside her. Soon all was still as the last of the pack ran from the stallion and the only things that stayed in that small opening was her, the deer, and the stallion.

Debace braced herself against the tree and pulled herself slowly up. She held her side and winced in pain as she tried to stand up straight. The stallion lowered its head and seemed to try to help her stand up.

"Where did you come from?" she asked as she stared at the beautiful stallion. She stood there, as if expecting an answer, and when no answer came, she went to the deer.

As she untied the knot on the deer's leg, Debace felt a breeze against her neck and heard a soft voice echo in her thoughts, "You called me," Debace spun around in surprise to find the stallion right behind her.

"I must be going crazy. Horses can't talk." She laughed at herself and finished freeing the deer.

The deer shook and sprinted into the field. Debace stood and looked down at her side to see the damage done. Her tunic was ruined. There was a large hole in the side and blood stained the soft leather. Debace lifted it to see what she had done to her side. There were many cuts and scratches, but nothing too serious. She touched it softly but quickly pulled her hand back as pained seared her side. She sighed and let her tunic fall back down over her side.

Then she finally turned back to the stallion and slowly walked over to it. "I don't know where you came from, but thank you. If you hadn't have come, this would have not been my only wound." She walked over to it and laid her hand on his neck.

The stallion bowed its head and Debace pet him softly. "I am here to protect you," Debace heard that same, calm voice echo through her thoughts. She gasped and stepped back, confusion clear on her face.

The stallion raised his ears and looked all about him, stepped towards her and seemed to bow before her, "I must go, my princess," And with that the stallion ran past her and disappeared through the field.

"How is it feeling?" Jonathan walked into Debace's room and saw her bruise. Debace jumped in surprise.

"It's just sore." She said as she smiled slightly.

Jonathan walked towards her and laid his hand right above the bruise. A blue light emanated from his hand and he closed his eyes for a moment. "Your rib has healed fine. I still don't understand how you broke a rib from falling. It just doesn't make sense." Jonathan examined her side.

Debace felt guilt envelope her, she did not like lying to her father but if he knew what had really happened he would never allow her to leave the house. "I need your help with the garden outside. We need to harvest the corn." He stated as he began to walk back out of Debace's room.

"Yes, Father. I shall be there in just a moment." Debace quickly put on her tunic, threw on some shoes, and ran outside.

Debace walked out of the house and looked around for Jonathan. It seemed that he had disappeared, but suddenly she saw him come out of the barn with two baskets.

Debace ran to him and grabbed a basket. She walked quickly to the garden and began to pull the corn from the stalks and stacked them in the basket. Jonathan watched as she worked quickly. He couldn't believe that it had already been 13 years since she had come into his care.

She grew very tall, taller than he was at least, and her long, dark brown hair flowed down her back. One thing that had never changed, though, was her eyes, that soft, caramel color, and every time he looked into those eyes he seemed to relax. She had grown to be a very beautiful young lady, with long, muscular legs and an hour glass figure. She had a strong spirit and an aura of happiness that emanated from her.

"Father, do you need anything from town?" Debace asked.

Jonathan looked up and stared at her blankly, still entwined in his own thoughts. "What? Oh, no, but you might ask Kendra if she needs something." He said, still in a daze.

"Ok, is Beauty in the field?" Debace asked as she set down her basket full of corn.

"No, she's still in the barn." Jonathan answered.

Debace picked her basket back up and walked quickly to the barn.

When she reached the large open doors, she set the corn on the ground and grabbed a saddle from the wall. "Hey girl, we have to go to town." Debace set the saddle down and patted the mare on the neck. Her beautiful dark black fur glistened and her long mane and tail seemed to float in the air. "You'll never believe what happened yesterday. I saw the stallion, the one from my dreams." Debace said as she put the saddle on the horses back.

She began tightening the straps when Beauty began to become restless. "Whoa girl, what's the matter?" Debace grabbed the reigns and halter and put it on the mare's head, calming her down. "He talked to me, Beauty. How is that possible?" Debace patted Beauty on her neck and put her foot in the stirrup, about to jump on the mare's back.

"It's simple; I just never did before because I promised Satuu," Debace heard a woman's voice ring in her thoughts.

She pulled her foot out quickly and swung around. "Who's there?" Debace's voice shook with fear.

"Don't be scared Debace. It's me, but my names not Beauty. Although I do like that name, it's actually Quintara," The mare walked up to Debace and whinnied softly.

Debace stepped back slightly, her emotions playing fiercely on her face. "I don't understand. How is this happening? If you could speak to me all along, then why didn't you?" Debace walked up to the mare.

"I promised. It was necessary to protect you," Beauty's voice echoed through Debace's mind again.

"Why does everyone keep saying that?" Debace said aloud, but more to herself than to the mare.

"Aren't we going somewhere?" The mare asked Debace inquisitively.

"Yes, town, we have to stop by Kendra's before though." Debace said, still a little confused as she jumped onto the mares back, landing gracefully.

"So, what do I call you then?" Debace asked slowly.

"Beauty is just fine," the mare replied as she quickly galloped out of the barn and onto the long dirt road.

Chapter 16

Dust flew past Debace's face and stung her eyes as the mare galloped down the road, gliding through the air. Debace raised one hand up to shield her eyes from the dust and loosened her grip on the reigns, tightening her legs in the stirrups around the horse's belly.

Her thoughts were in chaos, trying to interpret the events that had unraveled before of her. She felt the wind blowing at her tangled hair, the tie that held it up loosening until it finally just fell, her long, rich brown locks blowing wildly in the wind.

Debace moved her arm from in front of her eyes as the wind began to die slowly down and the dust began to settle back to its resting place. She looked around with a puzzled look at the trees that surrounded them and the long, red dirt road that continued in front of them, seeming to go on for miles. She looked behind her at the bright path from which they had come, seeing nothing but dust floating in the air.

"Where are we?" Debace said aloud, slowly taking in every unfamiliar detail. The trees beside seemed to breathe, closing softly around the inhabitants of the road and then leaning back into the forest behind, and the never-ending road, a path that Debace had never seen before.

"Beauty," Debace looked down at the back of the mare's neck, worry clear in her voice. What was going on? Why were they here?

Debace felt a brush against her thoughts and she tensed, not familiar with the feeling. The mare started a bit, restlessly pawing at the ground and throwing her head one way and another.

Debace grabbed onto the reigns, her muscles tensed and her mind swarming with confusing thoughts. She patted Beauty's neck, attempting to calm her down.

Panic soon ran through Debace's thoughts as she felt that same sensation, as if someone was brushing softly against her thoughts. She kicked Beauty softly in the side and clicked loudly, trying to make her respond and take them away from this unfamiliar place but the mare wouldn't budge.

Debace tugged hard on the reigns and gasped as the sensation came back. She closed her eyes tightly, trying to clear her thoughts or block out whatever seemed to want in. Soon it went away and Debace quickly jumped off the horse's back and tugged hard on the reigns, patting Beauty and assuring her that they didn't need to be here.

When Beauty would not budge, Debace sighed loudly and looked deeply into the mare's eyes. "Why are we here?" Debace stood there, inches away from the mare's face, waiting for the answer patiently.

"You mustn't fight it, my princess," Debace heard Beauty's soft voice echo in her thoughts.

"Fight what exactly? I don't even know where we are! I think I've been patient enough with all of this! I just found out that horses can TALK! And a stallion that only appears in my dreams is now here in real life. That can't be a coincidence! Something very strange has been going on and I don't particularly want to know what it is. Why wouldn't my father have told me about all this? And why do you keep calling me *princess*?" Debace thrust her hands into the air as if begging for the answer to her questions to fall into her arms.

When it didn't, she lay her arms at her sides and plopped herself onto a large boulder beside the road. "I know you're confused. Not many people know of us, not even Jonathan. It has been that way for many years; it is the way we have survived. But answers will soon come, my pr..."

Debace had closed her eyes to concentrate on the words that were floating into her thoughts, and when it stopped so abruptly, she quickly opened her eyes and walked to Beauty who turned and began to walk towards the other side of the road. "What were you going to say? Why can't you just answer my questions?" Debace grabbed onto the headstall and begged for something to help her understand these things that were suddenly revealed to her.

Beauty let Debace pull her back to the middle of the road and submissively let her stroke her head. "Beauty, what is going on?" Debace said sternly, yet her voice shook slightly with the fear of the answer.

Beauty bowed her head down and sighed, her frustration clear. "Where is he?" Debace heard, yet this time it seemed distant, as if it wasn't meant for her.

"WHO?" Debace demanded. Beauty looked over at her quickly, her face scrunched into a confused look.

"What do you mean? How did you know I said anything?" Beauty walked over to Debace, her big brown eyes staring down at her, seemed to see more than just her face. They seemed to look into her soul and her thoughts, and Debace quickly tried clearing her thoughts, fear clear on her face.

"I don't know! I don't know anything anymore!" Debace felt tears well up in her eyes as she became more and more frustrated. She loosened her grip on the headstall and walked slowly back to the boulder she had sat upon before.

When she finally reached the boulder, she slowly climbed up onto a flat spot and sat, pulling her knees to her chest and wrapped her arms tightly around them. Tears began to roll unceasingly down her cheeks and she softly rocked herself back and forth, trying to clear her head. "I'm so confused," she whispered, her voice cracking as she sniffled slightly.

Debace looked up as she heard the sound of Beauty walking up to her and was greeted by her soft head comforting her, softly touching cheek to cheek. Debace raised her hand, rubbing Beauty's neck and leaned into her comforting gesture. Soon Debace had recovered herself and quickly she put her emotions in check. She had never had a problem with controlling her emotions and she would not start now. As she pulled away from Beauty and wiped her bronze cheeks dry, she stood sniffed loudly and relaxed her legs on the boulder. "So are you ever going to answer my question?" Debace said slowly, pronouncing each syllable deliberately, hoping that maybe if she made the sentence obvious then she would get some answers. Debace waited as patiently as she could, trying as hard as she could to cover the emotions that she knew played obviously on her face.

Beauty snorted out a long sigh and looked anxiously around her, searching through the trees. Debace tried to follow her gaze, trying to find what made her so anxious but when she could not, she began to stare once again at the black mare. "Beauty?" Debace croaked out as she watched the mare's eyes widen and she began to throw her head up, beginning to back away from Debace.

Debace listened intently, searching for that same calm voice to echo in her thoughts as it had before.

Beauty let out a loud whinny and pawed at the ground loudly. Debace watched Beauty as the look of distress spread from her face to the rest of her body, every muscle tensing. Debace spun around, suddenly feeling as though her throat were closing, cutting off her air supply, as she felt that same brush against her conscience, only this time it wasn't just her mind, it was her whole being.

Everything seemed to push against her body, and her breathing soon became short and fast, no matter how hard she tried to calm herself. She searched the trees around her, trying to find the source of her and Beauty's distress. She flinched as she felt the brush against her, stronger than before. "Beauty, what is happening?" Debace coughed out as she tried to catch her breath once more.

She turned around slowly when Beauty did not answer and watched as calm seemed to envelope the mare, her head slightly bowing down towards the ground.

"Beauty?" Debace could hear her voice tremble with the fear she knew played plainly on her face.

Her heart beat heavy beneath her chest, filling her ears with a steady thumping, or was that her heart at all. She raised her hand to her chest and waited, listening to the beat that filled her ears and feeling her own heart thump hard beneath her sternum, both out of synch. She gasped slightly, her heart fluttering now, searching around her for the source of the steady beat that became louder and louder, filling her ears and vibrating through her body.

"What took you?" Debace heard Beauty's voice echo softly in her thoughts. She swiftly scanned the trees beside her as the sounds became unbearable, turning hesitantly behind her when the sounds began to slow and became softer.

There, before her eyes, was a huge herd of dazzling horses. Every type of horse, from a bay to a chestnut, from an Appaloosa to one beautiful black horse, standing in the back, all stood before her, taking her breath away because of the beauty and grace that radiated from each horse.

She tried to step forward, to touch what she thought could only be a dream before it disappeared, but her feet would not move. Instead, she stood there in awe, mouth gaping open, and her heart beating beneath her chest, begging to be free. "How... Where..." Debace tried to stutter out, but her mind was still in shock and she couldn't concentrate enough to wrap her voice around the words.

"Debace, this is why we are here," Beauty explained softly.

She turned her head slightly, her mouth still gaping open, just enough to see the mare in her peripherals, and slowly turned her head again to gaze upon the herd of horses. It was as if every dream that had ever woven through her sleepless nights was suddenly before her, very obviously in her new reality.

Soon each horse began to separate from each other, making way for something Debace could not see over the majestic herd. As the horses began to separate even more, a glowing emanated from behind, causing Debace to gasp slightly as she squinted hard to see what was hiding behind the many horses.

"Could it be?" Debace whispered, more to herself than anything, when from behind the herd came that same stallion that ran through her dreams, and just recently through her reality, daily.

The radiant, white stallion walked slowly from between the front two roan mares to Debace, stopping just before her and bowing his head toward the ground as Debace had seen Beauty do earlier.

Debace wanted to scream, to ask every question that ran frantically through her thoughts, but all she could muster was a heavy sigh. It was as if the beauty and mystery of this stallion had run off with her voice, like in many of the dreams that haunted her.

Debace felt tears pushing at the rims of her eyes and blinked hard, letting the tears fall quickly as she waited for her body to react to her brain's commands.

"My princess, why do you cry?" Debace heard a strong base voice echo confidently through her hectic thoughts. Debace gasped and shook her head slightly, trying to clear her thoughts.

"I... Well, I don't know." Debace stuttered out as she giggled to herself slightly, realizing how ridiculous she must look. She felt her face heat up with embarrassment as she tried to recollect herself, attempting to keep her emotions carefully under control.

The stallion stepped forward, inclining his head to Debace, looking deep into her eyes.

"Where did you come from?" Debace asked, still a little breathless.

"We've been here all along, my princess. Always here to protect you," she heard the confident voice that she assumed must belong to the beautiful white stallion that now stood in front of her. She took a step forward, extending her hand to run it down the stallion's neck.

The stallion succumbed to her gesture, never exhibiting the restlessness that Debace feared her gesture would instill. She rubbed softly down the side of his neck, feeling the perfect musculature underneath the beautiful white fur.

She began to run her hands farther down towards his withers, carefully noting each detail, the beautiful, white fur, the silvery white mane, and continued down the back to his hips. To what she could see, this horse was perfect. She ran her hands slowly down the stallion's legs, careful not to make any sudden movements that would send the hoof flying towards her face. Once again, it was perfection.

The muscular leg led to a perfectly healthy hoof, and as Debace glanced at each hoof from her view point, she realized that everyone was just as perfect. There were no cracks or chips to be seen and the whole hoof looked as if it had been soaked in some kind of supplement.

Debace stood up straight, to behold the full beauty of the stallion and the whole herd once more. Then she turned back to the stallion, "What is going on?" she asked, desperate for some kind of answer.

"We are your protectors, and we have waited many years for this day, the day that you can learn of the Wild Horses," The stallion lifted his head and nodded towards the rest of the herd.

Debace stared blankly at the herd, confused, "I didn't know such a beautiful herd still existed. Didn't the emperor wipe them out?"

The stallion whinnied softly and stamped the ground. "He will never be the Emperor! He has caused nothing but chaos! He has tried to kill us off, but failed many times. We went into hiding, all the while securing the princess, the one who will forever right all wrongs." Debace heard the frustration and venom leaking through the words and flinched slightly at the sound.

"But father said that you were nonexistent! How can this be happening? And what are you talking about? Who's this princess I keep hearing about?" Debace could feel the questions flow out, as if a waterfall had been unleashed through her mouth. She quickly closed her mouth, not wanting to ask too much, but still waited a little too impatiently for the many answers.

Debace furrowed her brow in frustration when the stallion took too long to answer.

"Satuu, don't make this poor child wait any longer than she must." Debace gasped as she heard a soft voice of a woman, and a tear rolled down her eye.

"Who said that?" she demanded, desperate to find the owner to the voice. She recognized the voice from her dreams, that same comforting voice that always seemed to save her from her nightmares.

The black mare from the back of the herd stepped forward and wrapped her neck around Debace. "My child, it is time you knew your past." She said and back away slowly.

Debace turned to face the stallion, which the mare had called Satuu and waited for her answers.

She watched as Satuu stepped aside to reveal to her a small, fragile man. Skeletal like, his skin hung loosely on his bones, his long white beard hanging down in front of him. He carried a large staff at his side, which he handled with great care.

Debace backed away in horror. "No, it can't be. You aren't real!" she screamed as she recognized this man from her nightmares. She blinked vigorously, waiting for him to disappear as he had always before, but when he didn't, she merely stood there helpless.

She wanted to turn and run, to escape all of this that seemed so unreal, before one of her worst nightmares came true, but she couldn't.

The mare had said, it is time you knew your past. What did that mean? Did all this have something to do with her bizarre memory lapse of anything before the age of 5? She watched as the skeletal man raised his large staff slowly, opening his mouth and yelling something, but she didn't hear. Yet, she remembered this from her dream; she knew exactly what he had said. "It is time!" the exact saying she had feared all this time in her sleep.

She watched as he brought his staff down hard to the ground and the things around her seemed to melt away. Visions of a beautiful woman and a strong man flashed before her and soon she realized who these people were, "Mother, Father!" she cried, her tears rolling continuously down her cheeks.

She waited helplessly as every memory that had ever escaped her flushed to her mind. Tears rolled even faster, seeing all the things that had left such an utter hole in her memories, reminding her of the terrible and wonderful things that she had once been through.

Finally, the rush of images came to a stop, and her memories were finally returned to her. After all the dreams, all the wonders, she finally knew why she felt so different. Yet, all of the excitement of the day had proven too much. As the images disappeared and she came back with the horses, she collapsed to the ground, a black oblivion enveloping her consciousness.

Chapter 17

"Why did you bring her here? This is reckless!" Debace heard a husky voice growl.

"I have my reasons, Damian. That's all I must tell you." She heard a man reply, his voice soft, not quite a whisper.

Debace tried to open her eyes to see the men that the voices belonged to but soon forgot the men. She groaned as pain shot through her head and she gritted her teeth against the pain.

"Don't you dare treat me like one of your helpers! I am not the one who brought *her* here! Do you know..."

"Shh! She's waking up!" the other man hissed.

Debace gasped when she realized who they were so worried about. She opened her mouth, about to ask where she was, when she felt a calloused finger against her lips. "Don't strain yourself; you've been through a lot." She heard the softer voice say.

She slowly tried to open her eyes, wincing as the pain shot through her head again. As the pain subsided, she tried once more, hoping to see who was with her. She didn't recognize either of the voices and she wanted to see if Jonathan was somewhere around.

She finally opened her eyes enough to see a man leaning over her. She couldn't really see that much in the dark, but his blazing blue eyes stared down at her with such curiosity that she wondered how bad she must look. She tried once more to open her mouth but gave up when she felt the twinge in the side of her head. She didn't want to get that terrible migraine again.

"Just sleep. You are well taken care of." The man said finally, as she attempted many times over to say something, anything. Debace closed her eyes obediently and let herself drift into unconsciousness, feeling her exhaustion overwhelm her.

Debace opened her eyes quickly and gritted her teeth, awaiting the pain that had before accompanied the gestured, but relaxed when it didn't come.

She stared up at the ceiling, an array of brown, black, and white pebbles. She gasped as she studied the stones, seeing the patterns that played out like a picture movie, beautiful scenes of *horses*.

Suddenly, the memory of the Wild Horses rushed back into her mind and with it, the memory of the skeletal man. She stiffened as the unfamiliar memories started to flow through also, molding themselves in her thoughts and memories as if they belonged. She felt tears roll uncontrollably down her cheeks as she remembered something she had tried to remember her whole life.

"Father," She whimpered as her tears began to flow like a waterfall. She clenched her hands into fists, tightening her eyelids as the tears overflowed. All this time, that feeling of emptiness, was now filled with sadness.

Finally, the tears began to slow, and soon stopped. Debace wiped her cheeks with the back of her hand, drying her face. She sniffled loudly and tried to gather her emotions.

"How are you feeling?" she heard a low, male voice ask softly. She looked up quickly, startled, and squared her shoulders, straightening her back when she realized that she had not been alone.

"Who are you?" she asked. She watched warily as the man walked to the cot she sat on and sat beside her, quickly scooting over, hoping she hadn't made it too obvious.

The man let out a low chuckle, "You don't have to worry, if I wanted to hurt you I would have just left you out there." He gestured out the door, where Debace could see nothing but darkness. But she knew what lurked in the darkness; she had seen it many times.

She shuddered at the thought of waking to wild animals sniffing around at her or, even worse, ravenous animals gnawing at her limbs. "I suppose so." She whispered, her voice cracking when the images flew past her eyes as she thought of all the possibilities.

Soon, Debace remembered her new memories which she had just finished crying over. She remembered her mother, her beautiful eyes, and pictured her face for a long moment with her eyes closed. She felt a lump in her throat, and trying to avoid losing control of her emotions again she swallowed hard and cleared at her throat to occupy herself.

Suddenly a terrible face came through her memories, and she flinched, opening her eyes quickly to avoid the grotesque face distorted with hate. "Sou Harra," She gasped as she remembered who the man was and what he had once tried to do.

She felt a hand on her shoulder and recoiled, the face of Sou Harra still in her minds eye. She quickly softened her expressions when she remembered that the man was still sitting beside her.

"Oh, sorry," She said, startled at the look of concern on the man's face. She quickly worked at replacing her features with a mask of emotionless indifference. "You never told me your name." She stated.

She marveled at the strength in her voice as the thought of what the horses had told her before crossed her mind. "Princess," she thought breathlessly. A frown distorted her beautiful features. "Impossible, there must be some mistake." She reasoned, waiting impatiently for the man to speak.

She watched his face as he took a deep breath, as if preparing for a long story. The man's compassionate features twisted into a frustrated look and he straightened his back. "My name is Brian." He said, simply.

Debace exhaled, realizing that she had been holding her breath.

She searched her memories for the name, wondering if she may have known this man.

She opened her mouth to speak but the man raised a hand, stalling her. "Enough questions, you need to eat something." He said standing and reaching out his hand to help her up. Debace searched his face for something that would reveal to her who this man was, but when she found nothing she began to stand.

She soon felt very grateful for the man being so near as she felt her knees buckle beneath her as soon as she stood. "Whoa, easy now," He said, laughing lightly.

Debace glared up at him, and shoved his hand away, trying to stand up straight. The man chuckled and watched as Debace tried to straighten her legs and took a step. He was soon by her side as she felt her body fall towards the floor once more. "You have been through a lot. Let me help you." He said.

She finally caved and let the man grasp her waist, standing her on her feet. She laid her hand on his shoulder as he held to her waist and led her through the door way and to the right, into a brightly lit room. He pulled a chair out from the table and led her to it slowly, letting her fall into it.

Debace looked up at him, hoping that she looked grateful instead of angry. She quickly was distracted as she watched the man walk over to a small stove and grab a stack of steaks from the top.

"Thank you." She said as he laid a small plate in front of her with a steak, finally hearing her stomach growling ferociously with hunger. Debace stared down at the steak, feeling Brian's eyes on her the whole time.

"You must have fallen pretty hard to get that bruise." Brian said casually as Debace quickly devoured the steak.

"Huh?" she looked up, confused.

He pointed down to her side and she followed his gesture to the large bruise that lay from the encounter with the coyotes. She finally realized that she no longer wore the tunic and pants she had thrown on before, but shorts and a loosely fitting white shirt that didn't quite fall over her side.

She felt her aggravation etch into her features and tried to swallow down the anger that was boiling up.

"Where are my clothes?" she asked briskly, wondering who had changed her clothes for her. Brian gestured towards a cabinet with his free hand, a steak in the other, to a pile of dirty clothes.

"I had to check for injuries."

Debace felt her face heat up and she gritted her teeth. "You could have waited for me to wake up." She said, hearing the venom leaking through her voice.

"No I couldn't have. If I would have waited, then you could have died." He said, looking up innocently.

Debace gasped slightly, wondering at the extent of her injuries and how she had gotten them this time.

"Luckily there were none, so I just put clean clothes on you. And you're welcome." He chuckled.

Debace glared at him but tried to soften her features when a loud howl echoed through the house, remembering the visions of what could have happened.

"That damn dog! You know he hasn't left your side since I found you. I had to nearly fight him to get you in here." He stood and walked to the window, looking out at something in the night.

"What do you mean? What dog?" Debace asked, confused. Her hand hovered over her side, thinking of the fawn and all the coyotes who had tried to attack her before. And of the first time she had seen the white stallion other than in her dreams.

"Not the first time, though, just the first time in a long time." She reminded herself, thinking about the stallion's name. She stood slowly, her legs gaining strength, and she tried to walk over to the window beside Brian, aware at how unsteady her legs still were.

Brian turned around, watching Debace's weak attempt and walked to her to once again wrap his arm around her waist to steady her.

"I'm fine." Debace hissed through gritted teeth, unaccustomed to needing so much help. She shoved his arm away and straightened a little, concentrating on not looking too helpless.

Finally she made it to the window and she grasped the edge sturdily, steadying herself once more. She heard Brian chuckling behind her and frowned, staring out into the dark to distract herself as he came back to her side.

She squinted, trying to see the dog that he spoke of but couldn't see anything past the window. Soon, another howl echoed through the night and she jumped, startled by how close the sound was. She looked down, under the window, and saw a large coyote sitting there, staring up at her. She gasped and stepped back at the sight, still nervous from her last encounter of a coyote this size.

Her hand involuntarily flew up to her side and she stood there, trying to decide whether to look out again or not.

"My princess, I have come to protect you. Do not be afraid." Debace heard a soft, gruff voice echo through her thoughts. She quickly went back to the window, very aware that Brian was still watching her very closely.

When she looked out this time, the coyote was silently turned towards the window, still staring up at her. "A Protector," Debace whispered, hoping that Brian had not heard.

The coyote nodded once and bowed slightly up towards Debace. "For when the princess has returned," she heard the voice state softly.

"I should have known." She heard Brian's voice from behind her. She spun around quickly, fear closing her throat, as she contemplated whether he knew or even should know who she was.

Yet, instead of seeing a look of confusion or horror on his face, she saw a look of, well, remembrance.

"Known what?" Debace asked innocently. Brian looked at her with a smile, watching her feeble attempt at hiding her frantic thoughts.

"Debace, you never were good at hiding your emotions. I feel so stupid; I should have known why he was here. I just can't believe you're already 18."

Debace gasped, startled at how much this man already knew. She watched his face, searching for the answers in his features, in his bright smile that sent her stomach into summersaults.

"How did you know that?" she whispered slowly, "I just had a birthday a few days ago."

Brian smiled wider, making Debace feel those same unusual fluttering feelings in her stomach.

"You don't remember me, do you?" Brian asked his voice soft and reassuring. He took a few steps closer to her and slowly took her hand, looking deep into her eyes. "Think real hard, Debace. I had expected this, for your father never did like us playing together even when we were so young." He took her other hand and squeezed it slightly.

"My father," Debace whimpered, tears coming to her eyes as she thought of her true father, the one man who would not reappear from her strange past. She shook her head and tried to concentrate. Who was this man before her? He knew her father, and he claims to have known her, too, yet why couldn't she remember him.

She thought back into her recent memories, and soon came to her new memories or her old ones truthfully. She remembered her father, her mother, servants running around everyday, and a young boy, running through the courtyard with her, causing those same butterflies in her stomach.

Debace watched Brian's face closely, searching for any similarity with the boy and soon he smiled widely. "Adelbrian?" she asked, looking even closer at the now somewhat familiar face.

Brian nodded and let go of her hands, wrapping his broad arms around her.

Debace gasped slightly, unprepared for the familiar embrace. She struggled a bit, uncomfortable with the close contact, yet finally remembered how she had missed him, her old best friend, and hugged him back.

They stood there intertwined for quite some time, until Brian finally loosened his grip and looked into her eyes. "I've missed you." He said softly and raised his hand to her cheek, brushing away a lock of hair that hung loosely in her face.

"We all have. Now if you two are done, we must be on our way. We are not the only people in this land who have heard of our princess' return, and some aren't as happy as we." Debace jumped, startled by the new voice and turned around to see a tall, stout man, with dark hair and pale skin.

He had a large tunic on with pants loosely hanging on his large frame. There was slight stubble on his chin and above his upper lip and his eyes, a mixture of green and gold, were rimmed with thick lashes.

Debace watched nervously as he stepped through the door, her arms still wrapped around Brian, only too aware of what he meant by 'some aren't as happy as we.'

"Who are you?" she asked, her voice shaking a bit with anxiety. She tried to separate herself from Brian, but he only dropped one hand and tightly wrapped the other one around her waist. She struggled slightly to free herself and soon gave up, realizing how safe she felt in his arms. It was amazing what old feelings could do to you.

"My name is Damian Reubach. Brian and I have been searching for you for some time, my princess. He claims a white stallion told him where to look." Michael chuckled slightly, amazed at the thought of a talking horse. "Of course my friend is most mistaken. Everyone knows that horses can't talk, and those so gifted exist no more." He stated matter-of-factly.

"I wouldn't be so sure." Debace whispered as Damian walked away quickly. She watched the doorway he had walked through for a moment longer and turned to Brian, firmly grasping his hand and loosening his arm from her waist. "When did this stallion come to you?" she asked urgently, eager to find out as much information about this amazing creature that had saved her life and given her back her old life, however dismal that life might turn out to be.

She looked him straight in the face, grabbing his hands and squeezing them slightly and holding them close to her stomach, "Please, Brian, I need to know." She urged him, feeling desperation overtaking every emotion she felt. Brian looked down at her, a smile spreading across his face.

"I was walking the other night, looking up at the stars and around at the trees, and listening to the bustling sound of all the creatures of the night. It was peaceful, more peaceful than I had felt since you disappeared years ago and Sou Harra took over the Empire. Suddenly I felt an odd feeling, as if something was brushing against my thoughts, and I listened closely to the surrounding woods. Have you ever felt that feeling Debace?" Brian asked, pausing in his story, his eyes looking distant as he thought of what had happened.

"Yes, more than I would prefer." Debace replied. She walked slowly away from the window, where her and Brian were still standing and lowered herself carefully down on a seat that lay in the middle of the room. "It's as if nothing is private anymore." She whispered, more speaking to herself than to anyone else.

"Yes, well, it wasn't pleasant. Soon I could hear a soft beating on the ground, and as I listened closely I realized that it was hoof beats. Then I saw him. You used to speak of him when we were children. I remember you describing his beautiful coat and flowing mane and tail like it was yesterday. I stood, trying to decide whether I should stay or try to escape. That's when Satuu told me everything. About how Sou Harra had stormed the castle and how he had to practically drag you across the country, when finally you travelled on your own, and at such a young age." Brian sat beside her, turning towards her and watching every emotion playing across her face as if she had written it there.

He smiled slightly and went on, "When you had left, I hated every day that went by. I felt as if my life was not worth living, until Damian came into the picture. He had seen the whole thing, from you being dragged away to your mother's... Well he saw it all. And he told me you still lived and we still had a chance. Ever since that day we have been searching the lands high and low for you. And when the stallion came to me and told me of what was to come and how to find you, it seemed that it was really all worth while. As you have realized, Damian still thinks I'm crazy when I speak of the stallion, but you seem to believe me." He smiled from ear to ear, sending goose bumps up Debace's arms. She sat there, processing everything he had just said.

"So it's true. I'm not just going crazy, am I?" she frowned slightly, trying to make sense of everything. "I *am* a princess." She exclaimed uncertainly, feeling her heart flutter as she reached for Brian's hand.

Just yesterday, she was a poor farmer's daughter, and now, she finds that she is a powerful princess, who is destined to save an entire empire. This was a whole new chapter in her life, one she knew almost nothing about.

Debace looked up at the stars in the night sky, staring at those small, sparkling lights that seemed so far away and yet right upon them. She took a deep breath, tearing her gaze from the beauty of the night to a white stallion that stood on a hill in the distance, a herd of wild horses standing obediently behind it.

Wild horses, a beautiful and enchanting sight, yet for Debace, it was like a sight into her future. She was the princess, the one to right all wrongs, and she would do whatever she must to avenge her family's death.

CPSIA information can be obtained at www.ICGtesting.com
Printed in the USA
240220LV00002B/28/P